# RIGA

LUKE RICHARDSON

# 1

*1973, Latvia.*

Even before the clock reached midnight, Marija knew they wouldn't get out alive. Well, not all of them would get out alive.

Who would live and who would die? That was a decision she knew would come down to her. It was only fair, she supposed later. She was the one who'd got them into this mess to begin with.

It wasn't a decision any mother or wife should have to make. Marija wouldn't even wish that on her worst enemy.

Marija tried to push the malevolent thoughts away. She needed to focus. She needed to do whatever was possible to get them out alive. The feeling rose again, twisting like a knife thrust into her stomach. Someone was going to die tonight.

The hands of the clock on the dashboard of their ancient Moskvitch struggled towards midnight. The clock marked off the seconds in a series of electronic jerks; 57... 58... 59...

The car lurched and bumped. The night beyond the windscreen was clear and cold. The moon hung gaunt and pale in a featureless sky. Pine forests shivered on either side of the arrow-straight road. It hadn't snowed for two days, but drifts still nestled in the shadows where the weak winter sun couldn't permeate.

Marija peered up at the sky. They were unlikely to get snow tonight either. The sky was too clear for that. Then again, it wasn't the threat of snow that worried her.

She raised her gloved hands to her face and breathed into them. The warm air brought momentary relief from the biting cold. Her exhalation billowed out in front of her and condensed on the windscreen.

"Doesn't this thing get any warmer?" she said to her husband, beside her in the driver's seat. "I think it's colder in here than outside."

"No, that hasn't worked in years," Peteris replied, his eyes never leaving the road.

Marija glanced up at him. Like the moon above them, Peteris was gaunt and pale. The skin of his cheekbones, roughened by cold and blunt razors, was almost ghostly beneath the moonlight. Worry had made a permanent home around his eyes and long-since forced away the smile Marija had been drawn to all those years ago. Sitting there, the cold biting at her fingers, Marija tried to remember which had happened first; had the smiles stopped and then the worry moved in to fill the void? Or had the happiness been crushed out by the world around them?

Marija looked down at Peteris's hands on the steering wheel. For a moment, in the transient night, she swore she could see bone through his pallid and papery skin. Sadness clawed at her eyes. It's what this system did. It didn't fight you into submission, but it sucked all the fight from you until there was nothing left. Where there once had been passion, and joy, and life, now there was only skin and bone.

"How are they doing?" Peteris said, nodding towards the backseat. Marija turned. Andreja and Emilija, their daughters, lay curled up together. Two thick blankets shrouded them against the cold. Andreja, the older by two years, nestled into Emilija's shoulder. Marija couldn't help but smile. She would do whatever it took to protect her daughters.

Whatever it took.

"Sleeping," Marija said. "It's all a big adventure to them."

Peteris nodded, his eyes never leaving the road.

A tendril of mist swept across the tarmac, as though being pulled by an invisible hand. Peteris blinked for a full second.

"I can drive if you're tired," Marija said.

"No, it's fine," Peteris replied. "We won't be long now, another hour or so." He forced a smile and glanced at Marija. Deep lines furrowed his brow.

Marija looked at the clock. The hands now shuddered into the new day. A day that would change all of their lives forever.

# 2

*Present day, England.*

Andreja watched the ancient steeple of St Andrew's Church creep closer as they edged up the hill. The car smelled of furniture polish and flowers. The other occupants, friends of her mother's and who Andreja barely knew, talked quietly. It was the sort of inane conversation of which English village dwellers are world-class experts.

St Andrew's Church was as much a part of the landscape as the hills and fields that dominated this part of East Sussex. Andreja had passed it hundreds — no, probably thousands of times — over the last forty years. Today, though, it somehow looked different. Ominous, even. The ancient rock towered against the sky, as though destined to fall in on itself. Andreja felt as if it probably would. Nothing seemed that stable any more. Even the sky's arc of blameless blue couldn't penetrate her sadness.

The driver, dressed in black tails, slowed and turned the Rolls Royce into the lane leading to the church. Sunlight filtered through overhanging trees and dappled the car in a patchwork of light and dark. Her mother loved days like this. Even as the illness ravaged her mother's mind, she adored sitting amid the wildflowers of her garden, remarking on the insects and birds that made it their home too. Nature was her mother's one true friend. Her mother had no ill-feelings towards nature, as she seemed to with every human she came in to contact with.

"They were here before us," she'd say in their native Latvian, a bony finger pointing at some noisy bug or other. She would never speak to Andreja in English. It was as though Latvian was an umbilical tie between mother, daughter, and their homeland. Andreja wondered briefly if she would ever use her mother tongue again now. "And they'll outlive us too. You know how many insects die at the hands of each other?"

Andreja always shook her head. She knew the monologue word for word.

"None. Not one. They live in peace with each other. No need for anything else."

Although her mother's diagnosis had come nearly ten years ago, it wasn't a surprise. Andreja knew she hadn't been well for many years. The signs were there. She got confused and angry, often launching into long soliloquies which kept Andreja on the phone for hours. In the end, the diagnosis came as something of a strange relief. At least now they knew, even if the outlook was bleak. Andreja would always rather know.

In the end, Andreja made the decision to take a break from her doctorate and move back to the village. Even now, she didn't know if coming to watch her mother's slow decline had been the right decision. But it was what she had to do.

# 3

*1973, Latvia.*

Marija watched the hands of the clock tap out the passing seconds for a full ten minutes. The car wallowed through the dense blackness. The weak headlights cast a soft glow, illuminating the road only a few feet ahead. The Russian-made bulbs were no match for the night this far from the city.

"How long do you think?" Marija asked, her voice cracking against the cold.

"Half an hour. Forty minutes, maybe," Peteris replied, his eyes fixed on the road.

"We're cutting it fine. The boat leaves at one a.m., whether we're on it or not."

Peteris inhaled sharply. His eyebrows inched together. He held the breath for a moment and let it go. He further depressed the accelerator, and the pitch of the engine increased to a whine.

"We'll make it, don't worry," he said, his voice soft.

Only once in their relationship had Peteris raised his

voice. Marija couldn't even remember what it was about, but it had shocked her. It seemed to shock Peteris, too. He had apologised immediately and since that day had taken a deep breath before replying to something which irked him. Marija wasn't that virtuous. She flared up frequently, but always apologised afterwards.

"Mummy, mummy!"

Marija's reverie was interrupted by a voice from the backseat. She was so deep in her thoughts that it startled her for a moment. She turned to see Andreja rubbing her eyes.

"Where are we, mummy? I need the toilet."

Marija forced her expression into a smile and turned to face the child. Holding the smile in position felt like an exercise in contortion. Smiles didn't fit like they used to.

"We'll be there soon, baby. You're going to have to hold it I'm afraid, we can't stop here."

Andreja's face twisted into a snarl of discomfort. "I can't, I can't, I can't. It's coming, it's coming out now."

"We'll make the time up," Peteris said. "We're not far now."

"We shouldn't. I —"

"She'll wet herself and have to sit all night in those clothes. She'll freeze to death. It'll take less than two minutes." Peteris removed his hand from the wheel and placed it on top of Marija's. "It'll be fine. I'll keep the engine running. You jump out."

Marija looked at Peteris. He had always been a soft touch for their daughters, and they loved him for it.

"We'll be on our way in seconds."

Marija nodded. "Okay, hold it baby. We're stopping now."

The whining engine of the Moskvitch faded to a hum

and then an idle murmur. Peteris pulled onto the verge. Gravel crunched beneath narrow tyres.

Marija looked at him. Their eyes locked. For some reason, a reason Marija could not fathom at all, Peteris was smiling. It was the sort of beaming grin that had suited him so well many years ago. Maybe it was a trick of the light. The full moon did funny things to your eyes.

Marija scrambled out of the car. The cold hit her like a fist to the chest. She exhaled heavily and stamped her feet to get them moving. She opened the back door, flimsy hinges screeching loudly. Something scurried in the undergrowth nearby.

"Come on then, quickly now," she said, lifting the blanket and helping Andreja from the car. A gust of wind whipped at her face and threw the car door shut. Metal clanged against metal.

Andreja ran towards the thick, dark shapes of the pine trees.

"No, just do it here," Marija shouted. "We don't have time for this."

Andreja dissolved into the shadows. Marija huffed and trudged after her.

# 4

*Present day, England.*

The car slowed, gravel snapping beneath the wheels as it pulled to a stop behind the hearse at the church gate.

Andreja gazed out at the churchyard. Mourners moved between moss-covered headstones. Andreja couldn't help but be struck by the futility of it all. You'd end up in a place like this, whatever decisions you made. Yet, all you had in life were decisions. Decisions defined who you were and what you stood for. Andreja knew more than most about life-changing decisions. Not least, giving up her doctorate to help her mother in her years of need. She wasn't the sort of person who could ignore her mother when she needed help. Andreja's life came second. That was the way it had to be.

Andreja watched a man and woman walk beneath the church steeple's angular shadow. As they emerged back into the sunlight, she noticed the splash of colour from their lapels. Both had wildflowers pinned to their chests, a final request of her mother's. She glanced down at the flower pinned to her own dress. She'd picked it from her mother's garden that morning. Its blue petals, which looked so alive and vibrant amid the long grass an hour ago, looked bleak and deathly now. She regretted the choice. Maybe she should have gone for something red.

Andreja pulled a deep breath of the perfumed air and leaned back into the seat. She closed her eyes for a moment. Her mind spun in a maelstrom. She felt as though she hadn't taken a breath in weeks. In contrast to her mother's slow decline, what happened afterwards had been a whirlwind. There were arrangements to make and well-wishers to entertain; people who hadn't been interested when her mother shouted obscenities at anyone nearby now wanted to talk about what a great woman she'd been. And now here she was — a heartbeat later — following her mother's final journey.

Her emotional typhoon raged on. She let the breath go. A gloved hand touched hers.

Andreja opened her eyes. The woman beside her smiled in that grief-stricken way people do. Andreja returned the expression as best she could.

The driver opened the door. The oppressive temperature of the summer heat-wave streamed in. The heat had arrived ten days ago and showed no signs of letting up yet. Andreja glanced up at the cloudless sky. Sweat prickled her forehead. She looked in the direction of the sea in an attempt to avoid watching the coffin-bearers slide her mother from the hearse. From the cottage this morning, the waves had looked like a bed of sparkling diamonds. It was too far to see from here. A hot stream of air shook her back into focus. She gave in and looked towards the hearse. The coffin-bearers lifted her mother to their shoulders. Then, with practiced efficiency, they started in the direction of the church.

Andreja looked up at the dazzling sun. At least it was the sort of day her mother would have loved.

The tempest within Andreja's mind continued as the funeral passed in a blur. The priest read a eulogy of a life well lived. He spoke of her work at the University of Latvia, before her secondment to Canterbury, where she stayed for the rest of her career. He boasted of her undying interest in international politics, shared by her only surviving daughter, Andreja.

"Lovely service. I'm so sorry for your loss," a man said as Andreja walked towards the exit. Andreja smiled vacantly in response. It wasn't unusual for her not to know who people were. She'd spent most of her time here caring for her mother. She hadn't gotten to know the community. People seemed to know who she was, though.

They paused behind the coffin as someone opened the doors. Andreja inhaled a deep breath of the church's ancient air. The doors swung wide and a thick bar of sunlight streamed in. Dust motes whizzed like shooting stars.

The coffin-bearers shuffled on.

Andreja followed her mother out into the dazzling sunshine for the final time.

## 5

The New York afternoon air was heavy and cold. Leo took a long breath. It slipped deep into his lungs. It revitalised and energised him. He gazed up at the surrounding buildings. A thousand windows glinted in the bright winter sun.

The familiar squeeze of anxiety pinched his chest. But this wasn't the anxiety he feared. This wasn't the anxiety that could leave him a quivering mess for days on end. This was a nervous, excited energy. It coursed and bubbled through his veins.

He looked over at Allissa standing beside him. Her smile was warm. Her eyes beckoned him close. Their hands fell together like the last leaves of autumn. She was the woman he'd literally followed to the ends of the earth. He couldn't imagine their lives apart.

In his mind's eye, the final scene of a movie played out. The strings rose to their climax; the camera zoomed out, and dust danced in the projector's beam.

Leo leaned forward.

Allissa's lips parted to greet his. The kiss — their first

kiss — was soft, passionate and longing.

He was kissing Allissa, and she was kissing him back.

"I love you," Leo whispered, his mouth an inch from her ear.

"Sorry, what did you say?"

Leo shook his head. The image drained. He stared dozily around their flat's front room. Through the window, the sky was a crisp, deep blue, the sun unyielding. The air in the room was hot and thick.

"I... nothing, I don't think," Leo mumbled, turning to face Allissa. His face flushed bright red.

Allissa sat on the sofa, working on her new laptop.

"You definitely said something," Allissa said, her eyebrows arched.

"Nope, nothing at all. You're hearing things." Leo pulled the front of his t-shirt away from his chest. "Is it just me, or is it getting even hotter in here?" He snatched up a magazine and fanned himself. "Forget heading south, it's hot enough here right now."

Six months had passed since Leo and Allissa had returned from New York. After a densely scheduled series of jobs had taken them to Kathmandu, Hong Kong and Berlin, they had decided they needed some time off.

For one, there was work to do on the business behind the scenes. Leo and Allissa both also wanted to spend more time reconnecting with their families. And, since the whole nature of their relationship had changed, they wanted to spend time together without being chased by bad guys.

Leo had enjoyed it. He'd quickly fallen into the routine of running every day, checking for new work, making sure things he'd handed on to other investigators were progressing, and whiling away the evenings on the sofa with Allissa.

For Leo, it was perfect.

*It's perfect because of her*, he thought, glancing over at Allissa.

6

*1973, Latvia.*

"Come here now," Marija barked into the darkness.

"I'm just going to the toilet mummy," came Andreja's voice in reply. "I can do this on my own now. You know that."

Despite the nerve-wracking fear, Marija felt a sudden jolt of pride and joy. How had Andreja grown up so quickly without her even noticing? She was fast becoming a young woman with her own thoughts and opinions.

"Okay, but make it quick," Marija said, much more softly than she'd intended.

Sharp headlights illuminated the trees from the direction of the road. A sickening sensation rose in Marija's throat. Her heart pounded like a machine gun. Her eyes searched the forest, instinctively looking for any sign of Andreja. The trees' angular shadows swirled and swung against the incoming lights. Marija saw Andreja, ghostly in the gloom. Marija placed a finger against her lips and beckoned Andreja close. They pushed back further into the undergrowth and turned towards the light.

The twin beams of an approaching vehicle lanced down the road, severing wreaths of fog and piercing through the trees. Marija's senses entered high alert. They hadn't passed another vehicle since leaving Riga.

The distant hum of an engine grumbled above the conspiratorial whisper of the pines. It was deeper, more guttural than that of a car. Marija held Andreja's hand tightly, all thoughts of the cold now forgotten. From within the trees, she couldn't yet see the approaching vehicle. She watched Peteris closely. He squinted in the Moskvitch's rearview mirror. Strong lights shot through the small car and patterned across his face. He glanced to the right and stared deep into the woodland, perhaps searching for Marija.

Whether he saw her or not, Marija wasn't sure, but his gesture was clear — a shake of the head.

*Danger. Do not return.*

"What's happening Mummy?" Andreja's voice was frail, almost otherworldly.

Marija tried to speak. Fear laced her voice.

"We need to wait for this truck to pass, then we'll get back to the car."

Andreja nodded in reply, pushing closely beside her mother.

The thump of the truck's engine drew closer now. Marija listened closely, hoping to hear no change. She prayed silently that it was a freighter en route from one of the farms, or on the cross-country route to Ventspils. Anything but that which she feared most of all.

A gust of wind charged through the forest. Distant

branches whooshed and creaked. An owl nearby called to an unseen mate. To Marija, it sounded like a cry for help.

The truck's lights grew in intensity.

Marija took a step backwards, tugging Andreja to follow. They crouched behind a bush. Marija pulled a deep breath. The fresh taste of cold night air and the tang of pine lingered in her nose. It was a smell she knew she would remember, one that would stay with her until the day she died.

Then, almost imperceptibly at first, the truck began to slow.

## 7

"What're you doing?" Leo asked, turning to face Allissa on the sofa. Whereas the heat aggravated Leo, a film of sweat constantly coating his body, Allissa glowed in it. She wore the bright clothes she'd collected on her travels and basked in the warmth. Leo fanned himself with anything to hand and took several cold showers a day.

Allissa looked up from her laptop. "That computer course I told you about."

"Hacking?"

"It's not technically hacking, although that's a part of it. You know, we're lucky we haven't needed anything like this before. As encryption becomes more sophisticated and —"

Leo yawned and turned towards the window. The opening mechanism of the ancient window was broken, so Leo had propped it open with books. The occasional gulp of air trickled in.

"And that's exactly why I need to do this," Allissa said, a scornful expression on her face.

"What?" Leo said, covering his mouth. "Sorry. I'm just... it's so hot."

Allissa rolled her eyes. "When we get a case that involves us needing to do something with computers, you'll be calling for me. And maybe I won't help you."

"What, you'd leave me to suffer alone?" Leo said, struggling to his feet, then crossing to the sofa and sitting beside Allissa. "To be fair, I managed alright without you in Berlin."

"No you didn't!" Allissa laughed out loud. "You'd be dead if it weren't for me."

"No way. Show me what this is all about?" Leo glanced at the screen.

Allissa started to explain the process she was working through.

Leo's eyes glazed over and then drifted around the room.

"Nope, you've lost me again. I'll just call you when it comes to computer stuff." Leo stretched backwards and rubbed his hand across his face.

"Any sign of a decent case yet?" Allissa asked. "We need to get out of here soon."

Leo grabbed his laptop and opened the lid. "Nothing that exciting. One woman whose husband's run away with the nanny."

"We could do that, easy." Allissa's eyes brightened.

"We could, but we don't do cases like that. He's run away because their relationship is over. We're not getting involved —"

"What if we run out of money?" Allissa said hopefully.

"Have we run out of money?" Leo asked. Providing their credit cards still worked and he wasn't hungry, the ebbs and flows of finance was largely a mystery to Leo.

"No," Allissa grumbled.

"We're not stooping down to cases like that, sorry."

Allissa stood up and walked to the window. A pair of seagulls pounded through the heavy summer air. "Don't you want to go out, though? Go and see places?"

Leo stood and shook his head. "Nope, when you're here, everything's great." Leo walked up behind Allissa and put his arms around her.

She moaned and exhaled. "Well, I do. If we don't find another job in a week, I'm phoning Nanny Lover and I'll go and find him myself."

Allissa shrugged off Leo's arms and stomped through the flat to the bedroom they were now sharing.

"I'd even do it for free," she shouted through the flat. "Just for entertainment."

## 8

*1973, Latvia.*

The truck's gearbox clunked and groaned as it slowed. The engine quietened from a menacing roar to an idle growl.

Clutching Andreja close, Marija peered out at the road. She willed her eyes to see more in the darkness.

The truck slowed further, brakes screeching and wheezing. The lights intensified. Finally, with an almighty shriek and hiss, followed by the clang of metal against metal, the truck juddered to a stop. The engine dropped into an idle patter. The lights continued to blaze.

Hidden in the shadows, it felt to Marija like a steel hand had reached inside her chest and clutched at her heart. She was frozen to the spot by fear, indecision and horror.

A door swung open. It creaked on decrepit hinges. A pair of boots crunched against the gravel. Two more pairs followed. Three figures emerged from the shadows and into the bright lights of the truck.

Marija gasped. A hand shot to her face. The steel hand

clutched harder at her heart, squeezing the life blood from her veins. Her head spun. Bile rose in her stomach.

Three men marched towards the Moskvitch, their rifles raised. One stayed at the rear of the vehicle while the other two fanned out either side. Their distant voices shouted for Peteris to switch off the engine and get out of the car.

Her brain registering the materialisation of her worst fear, Marija saw their uniforms. KGB.

Peteris stood slowly, his arms stretched upwards. He was deathly-pale beneath the truck's bright lights.

Marija choked back bile. Something inside shouted for her to move, to do something. Yet she stood motionless and obscured.

One of the men shouted, then led Peteris to the back of the car. Peteris quivered with a mixture of cold and fear. Marija could no longer feel the cold. Numbness consumed her body.

A man shouted again. Peteris pointed at Emilija, still asleep in the car. The man on the car's passenger side put down his gun. It swung on a strap across his chest. He flung open car's rear door, reached in and yanked Emilija from the back seat.

Emilija's frightened scream echoed through the forest.

The iron fingers clutched harder at Marija's heart. She pulled Andreja in closer beside her. What she saw now appeared as though from a nightmare. An awful, destitute nightmare, from which she knew there was no escape.

The man dragged Emilija to the back of the car and made her stand beside her father. The six-year-old girl was a picture of fragility next to the men and their weapons. She stood, visibly shivering, her teeth chattering in the cold night air.

A voice cut through the distant chugging of the truck's engine. It was deep and smooth.

"Peteris Panasenko."

The voice carried clearly through the still night air. The soldiers bristled upright, guns still aimed at Peteris and Emilija. Marija knew immediately who it was, even before he stepped into the light. Johanson Mikhail. The feared head of the Committee for State Security of the Latvian Soviet Socialist Republic. The leader of the Latvian KGB.

A figure sauntered from the truck and stepped into the light. He moved with the grace and strength of a big cat. Mikhail was a tall man, with long arms and hands that looked as though they could crush a man's skull. Unlike many leaders of his time, though, Mikhail wasn't a thug. There was intelligence in his dark eyes. Mikhail was equally at home in the dark cells of The Corner House — KGB HQ in Riga — the offices of governments, politicians and business leaders. The tools of his trade were blackmail, fear and brutality.

Marija's arteries and veins stretched and buckled under the pressure.

"Peteris Panasenko," Mikhail said, stepping up to the man. He was only slightly taller than Peteris. Peteris's body, though gaunt and malnourished after years of harsh rations, seemed insignificant by comparison. "It's so interesting that you should choose to go for a drive tonight of all nights. This far from home, too." Mikhail smiled, like a cat toying with its prey.

Peteris stuttered an answer, but the words were unintelligible.

"It's okay," Mikhail said. "Don't worry about it. I understand that sometimes it's nice to get out of the house, out of the city, you know? I do the same myself."

Peteris nodded. Then his head jarred backwards as Mikhail shoved him hard against the car. Peteris caught himself and struggled upwards. Emilija wailed, her voice cutting through the silence.

Mikhail turned his gaze on the girl. He crouched down and examined her tear-streaked face. "It's okay, don't worry, me and your daddy are going to have a little conversation. Is that okay?"

Emilija blinked several times, wiped her eyes, and nodded.

"What's your name?" Mikhail asked. Emilija answered between sobs.

Mikhail stood and turned his gaze back to Peteris. "It's interesting that you'd choose to bring your daughter out with you for one of your midnight drives. I wonder what we'd find if we looked in the back of the car. Just as a guess, I wonder if we would find some suitcases packed and ready to go?"

"I... no..." Peteris stuttered again. Mikhail held up a hand to stop him. One of the soldiers moved forward to open the boot. Mikhail stopped him.

"Maybe we'll look in there later. First, I want to have a conversation with my new friend Peteris."

The soldier stepped back.

"Now, to be honest, I have no interest in where you or your daughter are going at this time of night. Or, quite frankly, what you have in your car. Do you understand?"

Peteris nodded.

"But I do very much, with some urgency, want to have a conversation with your wife, Marija Panasenko."

Peteris stuttered again. Mikhail held up his hand.

"I don't want you to answer right now. I want you to think about this very carefully. Maybe you need some more incentivising." Mikhail drew a handgun from a holster beneath his jacket and levelled it at Peteris's head. "Now, I'm a very, very busy man. I really don't have time to be messing about. You either tell me the truth, in a moment, when you're ready, or you'll die. Do you understand that, Peteris?"

Peteris nodded. Emilija howled.

In the darkness, Marija stood frozen to the spot. She clutched Andreja to her. The young girl made no noise.

Marija's mind raced. If she revealed herself now, she would die, that was for certain. But would Mikhail spare the lives of her family? They wouldn't get out of the country, that was for sure.

"Okay, Peteris, I'm going to ask you a question now. You'll have one chance to answer me truthfully."

Peteris nodded.

Marija's heart thundered in her chest. It was less than ten miles to Ventspils. They could make it on foot. Or she could put her faith in the hands of one of the country's most brutal men. Marija pulled a deep breath and summoned every ounce of her courage. Steel ran through her veins. Mikhail was inhuman. He had no emotion. To escape from him, she would have to be inhuman, too.

"Peteris, where is your wife, Marija Panasenko?"

"I don't —"

A single shot rang out through the silent woodland. It was followed by the dull thump of Peteris's lifeless body as it fell to the gravel.

Marija didn't see a thing, though. With her face tensed against the cold, her lips set into a determined snarl and her hand locked with Andreja's, she pushed her way deep into the forest.

# 9

*Present day, Riga.*

The Commissioner of Police looked out at the waiting gaggle of journalists. He sighed. Internally, of course. He would never let the expectant cameras, or darting eyes fuelled up on free coffee, see how much he despised this unwashed hoard.

*I mean, look at you,* he thought, glancing down at a man he knew wrote for one of Riga's largest newspapers. The man's sagging body was forced into a threadbare jacket which could well have been in service since Lenin was a boy. By comparison, the Commissioner's suit, tailored in pinstripe grey, had been custom-made specifically for this occasion. He needed to look his best for this announcement. His pictures would be seen all over the country, possibly even the world.

"Thank you, ladies and gentlemen, for coming today," began the press officer. Her voice boomed through the room via the cluster of microphones crowded around the lectern.

Through the window of the conference suite on the

sixth floor of Riga's most expensive hotel, the city was bright but colourless. The spire of the Latvian Sciences Academy building looked like a melted candle on an impressionist's birthday cake. The heat-wave that had scorched Europe for the last few days had finally pushed its way to the Baltic coast.

The Commissioner stepped back beneath the stream of the air-conditioned air issuing from one of the ceiling vents.

"Our esteemed Commissioner of Police has a rather exciting presentation for you today —"

The door at the back of the room clattered open. The journalists turned as one to see which of their colleagues was unable to make the *prompt* nine thirty start time.

A young woman in, what The Commissioner assumed — and he had become something of an expert — her twenties, strode into the room.

"Sorry, sorry," she said, pulling a notebook from a satchel and taking a seat at the back.

The press officer grumbled before continuing. "He will outline..."

From the back of the stage, The Commissioner's eyes swept across the audience. His gaze returned time and time again to the woman at the back. His mouth twisted into a thoughtful sneer. Having a journalist on the inside might be just what he needed. He would have to give that some thought.

"Please save your questions until the end, when we will have a short time to answer them," the press officer droned on. "But for now, please welcome your Commissioner of Police, Johanson Mikhail."

## 10

*Present day, England*

Mervin Merrowford glanced up at the clock on the wall of his office. The hands struggled beyond nine thirty. He sighed; it was not going to be an easy day.

Climbing to his feet, Merrowford looked out at the mirror-flat surface of the English Channel beyond the window. He loved this view. It was the main reason he had taken the lease on this office all those years ago. He loved that from his rooms above a fish and chip shop in the old town area of Hastings, he could watch the weather roll past like crowded buses. From up here, the din of the town was muted too. The squawk of the gulls, or the rumble of the amusements, were nothing but distant whispers.

The oscillating fan stood on the filing cabinet creaked around to face him. He exhaled in the sudden blast of air.

The grandfather clock clanged. A seagull which had found some semblance of comfort on the windowsill pounded towards the fishing boats in search of a third breakfast.

The fan moved on and the air became stagnant again.

Merrowford dabbed his forehead and strode over to a large safe in the corner of the room. He removed the key from the inside pocket of his jacket and slid it into the lock. The ancient mechanism crunched, clicked, and then disengaged. Merrowford pulled open the door. The hinges screeched. He reached into the safe and removed a package that had lain untouched for more than a decade. Merrowford thought about it; closer to two decades.

He straightened up, his back protesting at the movement, and examined the package in his hands. He had never been comfortable with this case. There was something unusual about it, and it all hinged around this package. Merrowford had seen his fair share of strange posthumous requests, but this was entirely different.

He remembered the woman who had, some years ago — although it seemed like only last week — visited his office, anxious to write a will as soon as possible. She explained that she was in a rush because she feared she was losing her mind and didn't know how much longer she'd have the gift of rational thought. Merrowford had moved some appointments around and spent the morning re-drafting the lady's will, in which they'd set up a trust for her sizable estate.

But that wasn't the bit that troubled him. It was the strange terms of the will that all hinged around this package. Merrowford looked down at the brown paper covering. There was something strange and unsettling about this whole thing.

Merrowford crossed back to his desk and placed the package on the green leather inlay. He tried to swallow back his disquietude and grabbed the phone. He dialled the number of the detective agency a friend had recommended and turned towards the window. What secrets this package contained he didn't — and would never — understand. He was just following the wishes of his client.

## 11

Doing nothing was hard. Allissa looked up from her laptop and examined their flat's front room. The flat that she and Leo shared was at the top of a large Victorian house towards the Hove end of Brighton. Allissa gazed at the blue square of summer sky through the window. A seagull swished past, boasting its freedom.

In the six months since they'd returned from New York, Allissa had redesigned their company's website, caught up on all the admin, and now was trying to focus on her online computer course.

She looked at Leo, scrolling through online listings of cars for sale.

Leo, on the other hand, seemed totally at peace with a sedentary lifestyle. He seemed happy to pad around the apartment, read, go for afternoon runs by the sea and drink beer in the evening.

Allissa put her laptop on the sofa beside her and stood. She twisted her back and shook her arms in an attempt to loosen the frustration.

"What do you think about this one?" Leo asked, turning his laptop towards Allissa.

Allissa crossed the room and squinted at the car. It was some white shiny thing with sparkling wheels.

"It's alright," she said. "It's just a car, though, right?"

"Well," Leo said, leaning back in his chair, "this isn't really just a car. It's a BMW x5 with a —"

Allissa looked beyond Leo and out through the window. Traffic sat stationary in the street down below. One driver impotently protested on the horn. Fumes belched out into the air. Allissa considered for a moment why the hot weather made people so rude, then dropped the subject and tuned back into Leo's monologue.

"It's got a top of the range V8 and —"

"Oh right," she cut in. "A V8. That's sounds nice, but what does it do?"

"What do you mean, what does it do?"

"You tell me all these exciting specifications, so I'm assuming it does something more exciting than a car without all of those things, so what does it do?"

"Well, you know. You use it to drive places."

"Okay, like any other car then?"

Leo let out a long-exasperated breath and stared out through the window.

"I've never owned a car before," Leo said. "We work hard, and I'd like to have something that's nice. To be proud of, you know? Does that make sense?"

"Of course it does." Allissa patted Leo on the shoulder. "You can waste your money on whatever you like."

"It's not a waste of money, we'd use it all the —"

"What for?"

"Going places!"

"We're always going to places without one, so how's this

going to make a difference? I honestly have no opinion on this either way. It's your money, so spend it on whatever you like."

"But what do you think about it?" Leo scrolled to another page and showed Allissa an equally glitzy car.

"I think it's up to you."

"But I'm buying this for us, you know. It'll be ours to go to places we like."

"No, you're not." Allissa turned to face Leo. "I don't want anything to do with this. You're buying it for you. I like getting the train and I like spending time away from here. If you want to buy it, that's not a problem, but don't start bringing me into it. Plus, we live in a flat without a parking space. Where are you going to keep it?"

"There are a few places around here to park it on the street. We'll just have to move it every four hours —"

"I'm sorry, what?"

"We'll —"

"No way I'm touching that thing." Allissa waved her finger towards the computer. "You'll have to move it every four hours. I don't even want you putting me on the insurance of that thing. If you want it, cool, but it's yours."

"Okay, let me get this right. You don't like it because it's a nice car. Remind me what car you learned to drive in."

Allissa folded her arms. "That's not the point. It's not my fault my dad collected cars like other people collect —"

"What car?"

"A Land Rover."

"And how old were you?"

Allissa tapped her chin. "About fourteen, I think. It was on private land, around the lower field," she added, noting Leo's surprise.

"You can see the possible use in us having a car though, right?" Leo folded his arms now.

"No. It's been six months since we got back from New York and, quite frankly, I can't wait to go somewhere again. I mean, I like Brighton, but I don't want to spend every day of my life here."

"Exactly." Leo grinned. "We could go somewhere in the car. It would be perfect for day trips."

"That's not what I mean. I don't want a day out in Bognor Regis. I want to go and do exciting things."

"Like jumping out of exploding buildings?"

"Well not specifically that, although that was fun."

Leo scowled and turning back towards the computer. He clicked through a few more listings.

Allissa looked around the front room. The wallpaper looked even more discoloured than usual against the bright afternoon sun. She peered outside again. The traffic inched forwards another six feet. A man in a sports car with the top down leant on the horn.

Six months. That was the longest Allissa had spent in one place for years. The beat of curiosity and frustration pulsed through her. She needed to move.

"What about this one?" Leo said. "It's a fraction of the cost of that last one."

Allissa turned around to see some horrendous gold-coloured car on the screen. She raised an eyebrow and smiled. "And that's preferable to a train —"

Allissa's phone buzzed on the coffee table. She ran across the room and snatched it up. An unrecognised number scrolled across the screen.

"This could be a job." She glanced up at Leo, crossed her fingers and thumbed the answer button.

## 12

"It gives me great pride to tell you," — Mikhail paused and glanced at the gaggle of journalists waiting on his next word — "that, thanks in no small part to the initiatives I have led as Commissioner of Police, and of course the hard work of my fantastic officers, that crime in our great country continues to fall."

The expectant journalists let out a collective, impatient sigh. Having given up their mornings to attend a press conference by the Commissioner of Police, this was not what they were hoping for. Especially with an election on the cards.

"I'll give you some specific figures now, to illustrate how well we're bringing the criminals to justice, men who used to find employment for their criminality here." Mikhail fixed his eyes on the back wall. His voice was deep and sonorous. He tapped the button on the lectern and a screen filled with graphs and figures, illustrating a neat, downward curve. Mikhail spent the next few minutes explaining the specifics of each graph.

The once keen eyes of the waiting journalists darkened

with boredom. Glances towards the door became more frequent.

Mikhail pressed the button one more time, and the crest of the Latvian State Police filled the screen.

"Thank you for your attendance today," Mikhail said, without sincerity. "And thank you for helping us make our great country safer by the day." He nodded and smiled, then stepped back from the lectern.

"Mr Mikhail will take a few questions now," the press officer said, busting forwards. "Just for five minutes, though, as we're on a tight schedule."

The journalists shook themselves into focus, and a forest of hands shot up.

"Yes, you," Mikhail boomed, pointing towards the young female journalist at the back.

The rest of the journalists groaned. One even snapped his notebook shut and stashed it away in his threadbare jacket.

The woman rose confidently to her feet and pointed her ballpoint pen at the lectern.

"Thank you, Mr Mikhail." Mikhail smiled warmly. "You've shared a lot of important, and frankly impressive figures with us this morning," she said.

Mikhail nodded at the compliment. He shoved the press officer aside and stepped back up to the lectern.

A dozen bloodshot eyes rolled. One journalist let out an audible sigh, no doubt of the mind that his prepared question would have been much better.

"But what I want to know, and I believe several of my colleagues here would want to ask the same question, are you going to stand in the upcoming election for the next president of Latvia?"

Silence hung around the room for a moment, and then

chaos erupted. Journalists shouted further questions towards the lectern. The press officer held up a hand. The room simmered back into silence.

"I'll take this one," the press officer said. "This press conference is to discuss Mr Mikhail's work as Commissioner of Police. Should he decide to stand for the presidential election, you will —"

"No, I'll take this question." Mikhail's voice reverberated around the room. He shoved the press officer aside once again. "Thank you for your question, miss —"

"Lapina."

"Miss Lapina." Mikhail simmered and pinned a smile to his face. He straightened his jacket and stood as tall as he could. All the eyes in the room were alert now. Pens hovered and cameras rolled. "I'm pleased to officially announce today that, in fact, I will be standing in next month's presidential election."

## 13

Merrowford pulled up outside Marija's cottage. He pushed open the door of his fifteen-year-old Saab and scrambled out. When the Saab had been new, the air conditioning would blast luscious cold air. Now it barely even trickled from the dashboard's vents.

Merrowford turned to face the cottage and dabbed at his forehead with a handkerchief. Or maybe he was just more sensitive to things like that than he had been fifteen years ago. He attempted to pull the back of his shirt away from his damp skin. He clenched his shoulder blades together and wriggled.

The cottage looked beautiful beneath the clear summer sky. Bougainvillea wrapped the quaint home in a shimmering blanket of pink and purple. Birdsong floated through the still air.

Three days had passed since Merrowford had reminded himself of the details of the will, called the detectives and set up this meeting with Andreja. His feelings of disquietude had now turned to a sickening guilt. This woman had lost her mother. Now he was legally bound to be the barer of even worse news.

Merrowford swallowed, took a fortifying breath, then snatched up his briefcase and crossed the road. He unclipped the gate and walked up to the blue painted front door. He straightened his tie and rapped his knuckles against the wood.

Merrowford turned to examine the garden. Bumblebees busied themselves around a lavender bush, their humming filling the air like distant music. Beyond the road, the sea shimmered hazily hundreds of feet below. The door clunked open. Merrowford turned and smiled.

"Miss Panasenko. Good to see you."

Andreja wore her lack of sleep with dark patches beneath her eyes. Her short blonde hair, which was normally so well kept, hung dull and lifeless.

Merrowford smiled more brightly, as though trying to infect his client with his forced happiness.

"Andreja, please," she said, wearily moving aside to let the solicitor in. "You'll have to forgive the mess. In truth, I forgot all about our meeting today. So much to organise, you know what I mean?"

Merrowford hadn't seen Andreja in some time. Perhaps over a decade. He detected the slight hint of a Latvian accent.

"Andreja, then," Merrowford said, his English tongue labouring over the unusual sound.

"It's just And-Re-Ah." Andreja petulantly sounded out the name. "The j is silent."

Merrowford followed Andreja into the house and through to the kitchen, ducking twice to avoid low exposed beams. Bare wooden floorboards creaked beneath his feet. A clock ticked somewhere nearby.

Merrowford looked around the kitchen. Tasteful watercolours of local scenes covered white walls.

"Sit down, please. I'll make us some tea." Andreja gestured towards a large oak table. "I'm sorry. I won't be great company today. There's just so much…" Andreja's voice trailed off as she filled the kettle and clicked it on.

A black and white cat lay in a square of sunlight on the table. The cat raised its head and eyed Merrowford malevolently, as though it knew the news the solicitor was about to deliver.

Merrowford smiled apologetically, slid his briefcase onto the table, and then sat down. The cat laboured to its feet, stretched, and stalked off into another room.

"Thank you for coming," Andreja said. The kettle rumbled. "To be honest, I'm finding this all a lot to make sense of. Mother was such a secretive woman. I've no idea what to do with half her stuff." Andreja pointed at three bags full of clothes by the door.

Merrowford nodded in a way that he hoped would convey understanding.

"I mean, I can't just, you know — " Andreja gripped the kitchen counter. Her face flushed. The kettle hissed. She took a deep breath. "I can't just throw it away. Can I? That was her stuff. That's my mother, there." She turned and pointed at the bags.

Merrowford nodded again and prayed silently that Andreja wouldn't cry. It would be a lot more difficult if she started crying now.

"I know it's a very challenging time," he said softly. The words felt hollow, but he didn't know what else to say. "It'll get better, it'll get easier," he lied.

Andreja made two cups of tea and sat opposite Merrowford. Merrowford caught Andreja's eye and then looked away. He snapped open his briefcase and drew out some papers. "I am rather afraid, though," he said shakily, refusing to meet Andreja's intense stare, "that what I'm about to tell you may make things a little more complicated." Merrowford kept his eyes fixed on the papers in his hands. "Your mother's will is not a simple one." He cleared his throat. "Marija Panasenko's last will and testament. Here it is. Yes. Okay."

Andreja's eyes narrowed.

"I'll just... right, yes." The heat in the room intensified. Merrowford drew a handkerchief from his pocket and dabbed his brow before continuing. "Marija Panasenko's estate, which includes this cottage, Bangalore, Fairlight, several savings accounts and shares in multiple companies both here and in Latvia," — Merrowford paused, cleared his throat again, and dabbed once more at his forehead — "has an approximate combined value, taking into account current prices and exchange rates.... Well, of course, I can't guarantee the figure you'd actually be able to sell these for, and I'm not a financial planner either. I would certainly recommend you sought the help of a financial planner if you were to want to sell any of these assets, what with the complex nature of tax law."

Merrowford glanced up and caught Andreja's gaze. Her large blue eyes tightened to pin pricks. The gesture told Merrowford to get to the point.

"Yes, well, I would say... all of that notwithstanding... that the value of those assets, at the present time, would be around three million pounds stirling."

Andreja gasped. Her hands shot to her mouth. Merrowford glanced up from the papers.

"Are you sure?" she asked. "There must be some mistake. My mother didn't have that sort of money." Andreja's brow furrowed in confusion.

Merrowford dropped the papers to the table and wiped his hands on his trousers. "As you've said, your mother was a very secretive woman. She obviously knew how to look after herself, financially."

Andreja's mouth opened as if to say something, but no words came out. Her lips hung parted for some moments before closing again.

"Well, to be honest, I've seen all sorts of things as a solicitor these last thirty years," Merrowford twittered on.

"So, hold on," Andreja said, her hand crashing to the table. "As my mother's only relative, I assume she's left that to me?"

The unseen clock ticked from the hallway. One bird squawked, and another answered.

"Ahh, well. I'm afraid this is where things get rather more complicated." Merrowford dabbed at his brown again. "As I say, you see all sorts of things as a —"

"Mervin, get on with it, please."

Merrowford looked up from the papers and stared into the large blue eyes again. He swallowed the sensation of grit in his throat and then dropped the papers to the table-top.

"Several years ago, before your mother became ill, she came to see me."

Andreja nodded.

"And she said — this may sound a little bit, urrr, urrm, unorthodox — she came to see me, and she explained that she had a dream, a vision. Actually, I think the word she used was 'premonition.'" Merrowford's fingers became inverted commas.

Andreja listened in stunned silence.

"She explained to me that in this vision, you and your late father were there, but your sister Emilija was not. This led your mother to believe that your sister, Emilija Panasenko, is still alive."

Andreja's jaw hung limp. She took a long breath, then sat up straight. "My sister hasn't been seen since nineteen-seventy-three," Andreja said, her hands clenched into fists on the table. "She was taken. She was just a child. There is no chance, no chance…"

Merrowford caught Andreja's eye and wished he hadn't. He examined his hands and then shuffled the papers.

"I'm afraid that… I'm sorry to say that… I'm quite serious. Although, of course, visions from the other side aren't legally binding, someone's last will and testament is."

"What does it say?"

"Your mother has decreed that — " Merrowford rooted through the pile of papers " — the estate is to be put into trust, overseen by Mervin Merrowford, only to be released if compelling new evidence is brought to light about the whereabouts of, or the life and death of, Emilija Panasenko — your sister."

"Emilija has to be dead," Andreja repeated, standing and pacing back into the kitchen. "The woman's crazy. She lost her mind. This can't be happening."

"I'm afraid she made this decision before her illness," Merrowford said soberly. "I've no reason at all to think that your mother wasn't thinking clearly. She's actually been very thoughtful here. Fifty thousand pounds will be paid to you immediately to cover expenses. I have a cheque for that here." Merrowford pulled out a cheque and placed it on the table. "She goes on to say that if you take no steps towards finding her, or hinder the process in any way, as deemed by Mervin Merrowford, then the whole estate will be given to" — Merrowford cleared his throat — "The Latvian Socialist Party."

## 14

"This is crazy!" Andreja shouted, pacing from the table to the kitchen sink and back again. "She's left me with all this to sort out while I'm in danger of losing the house to the socialists?"

The black and white cat appeared at the door and stared into the kitchen. Sensing the tension, it sashayed away to find a warm place to lie.

"Emilija hasn't been seen in nearly fifty years! She was taken away by the KGB. She's almost certainly dead by now."

"I'm afraid that's not what your mother thought," Merrowford said, his palms extended in an attempt to placate Andreja. "She was adamant that —"

"If I were to do this, I've no idea where to even start. I've never looked for missing people before. What do I know about tracking people down?" Andreja turned and scowled at Merrowford.

"Well, your mother thought about that, too." Merrowford shuffled through the papers. "She has got you some —"

A knock echoed through the house. Merrowford

glanced at his watch and then looked towards the door. "I expect that's them now."

Andreja frowned, struggled to her feet and crossed into the hallway. Merrowford strode after her. The door's antique hinges creaked open.

"Allissa Stockwell and Leo Keane," Merrowford said, beckoning Leo and Allissa inside. "I'm told they're considered experts in this field. They've found several people in various different countries across the globe. I think if you've any chance here, they're the ones to help you."

Andreja followed the strangers back into her kitchen.

"Come and sit down," Merrowford said. He turned to Andreja with something of a smile. "We're all here to help you. We want nothing more than to see you succeed in this. I know it's been a big shock —"

"You know it's been a big shock?" Andreja snarled. "You've just told me that, despite the fact I've been looking after my mother for the last ten years of her life, cared for her every need, and now, unless I find someone who's probably already dead, I could get kicked out of my house?"

"In summary that's what the will says, yes."

"How am I even supposed to pay these two to help me?"

"That's been dealt with," Merrowford said softly. "Your mother was a very astute woman. I have a cheque here for them."

"But we won't find her" — Andreja was shouting now — "because she's dead, do you understand that?"

"Yes, I realise what you think you know," Merrowford said.

"What I think I know?!" Andreja glared at Merrowford. "What I think I know? Do you know anything about the country we grew up in? People there didn't play games. The KGB didn't run holiday camps. I spent nearly ten years looking after my mother and now I could spend the rest of my life looking for my sister."

"Listen, yes, I understand —" Merrowford extended both palms in placation and then dabbed at his forehead again. "But you are going to have to try. It doesn't say here that you have to actually find her. You just need to find new evidence, or at the very least just let these two experts do what they can to find her. That was your mother's dying wish."

"All the while, I live with the prospect of losing my home when they don't find anything?"

"No, well, I'm sure they'll come up with something that could count as —" Merrowford glanced back at the papers — "compelling new evidence."

Leo glanced from the solicitor to the enraged woman. "We can come back another time," he said, taking a step backwards. "It's no problem. When things have sunk in a bit. As Mr Merrowford says, we've got a year to do this. A few days, or even weeks, won't make a difference."

"No, no, please stay," Merrowford said. "There's something I have to give to you that may help you with the investigation. Mrs Panasenko asked for you all to be here for that."

Andreja, Leo and Allissa exchanged glances.

"Come, please sit down." Merrowford hurried around the table, pulling out chairs.

Leo and Allissa sat.

"I cannot believe this is happening," Andreja muttered, reluctantly joining the others at the table.

Leo and Allissa shared a curious look and then watched the solicitor.

"There is just one more thing," Merrowford said, taking off his glasses, cleaning them and replacing them on his thin nose. "Many years ago, Mrs Panasenko, your mother, gave me this for safekeeping." Merrowford produced a package wrapped in brown paper. It was about the size of a paperback book. He placed it reverently on the table between them.

Leo and Allissa gazed on, intrigued. The brown paper looked old. Marija Panasenko's signature was scrawled on the top along with the date — September $3^{rd}$, 1993.

"It's been in my safe for many years," Merrowford said. "I've no idea what's inside, but I've been instructed to give it to you now, as Mrs Panasenko believed it may be of help to you with the search. She believed that adamantly."

Andreja reached across the table and picked up the package. She pushed her thumb beneath the edge of the brown paper.

"Wait, wait!" Merrowford said, his hands outstretched. "The instructions are for you to open it after I've gone. Only the three of you shall know the contents."

Leo and Allissa glanced at each other again.

Merrowford stuffed the papers back into the briefcase. "Miss Panasenko, if you have any questions about what we've discussed today, then please don't hesitate to get in touch." He looked at Leo and Allissa. "I really hope you can find some answers so that we can resolve this quickly. Thank you all. I'll let myself out." With that, Merrowford darted in the direction of the door.

Leo and Allissa watched Andreja's thumb slip further beneath the wrapping.

## 15

"What were you thinking?" the press officer barked as she led Mikhail into the backroom. The door thunked shut and the noise of the impatient journalists sunk to a whisper.

Mikhail looked through the window. Six floors below, a blue and white tram clattered down the street.

"We've hardly even spoken about this," the press officer continued. "That was not the way we should be announcing your ambitions for the presidency. No one else has come forward yet, and you don't want to be the first." She paced from one end of the room to the other. "We need to think about this carefully. Maximise exposure. This is a very bad idea. Very bad."

Mikhail turned from the window. "Who do you think you are?" he barked, his eyes narrowing.

The press officer stopped, spun around, and glared at him. "I'm the person who keeps you in a job, that's who." She pointed at him across the room. "I'm the person who makes sure your image stays clean. I make sure none of the stupid things you do get out there. You have no idea how hard I work for you. And you just dropped this on me."

Mikhail paced across the room like a big cat closing in on its prey. He got in so close that his face was just an inch from hers. "You do not get to tell me what to do, do you understand that?" He pointed at the door behind them. The sound of clearing furniture and idle chatter streamed from the conference room. "I'm the person those people want to speak to. It's my thoughts they care about. I'm the one who has brought them safety and employment, not you." He planted a finger on the woman's chest. "If you ever criticise me again..." Mikhail shoved her backwards, snarling. She thumped against the wall. "If you ever criticise me again, you won't just be out of a job. Do you understand me?"

The press officer looked at Mikhail through wide eyes. "Do you?" Mikhail shoved her again.

She whimpered softly, nodding.

"Good. Now go and a write a press release. I've announced I'll be running for president." He turned back towards the window. "This is great news for the country. I want it on every station by the lunchtime bulletin."

## 16

A large ginger cat stalked through the garden and paused to peer in through the open patio doors. Its attention was drawn momentarily by three people sitting at the table, then it turned to follow a butterfly skipping on the breeze.

Andreja tore away the brown paper carefully. Leo and Allissa sat opposite, watching in enraptured silence. The thirty-year old adhesive resisted Andreja's attempts to separate it for a moment, before splitting open. Andreja laid the brown paper out flat and peered at the contents. She looked up at Leo and Allissa, but didn't say a word.

A battered notebook bound in black leather sat on the table. The cover was unmarked, the pages yellowed and dog-eared.

Andreja pulled the brown paper from beneath the book. A sheet of notepaper slid out.

Leo and Allissa sat motionless. It felt as though touching the book, or speaking at this time, could somehow disrespect the memory of Andreja's mother. The silence of a séance settled over the kitchen.

The anger had drained from Andreja's expression now. Her large blue eyes blazed with intrigue. She examined the brown paper carefully, folded it once and then laid it to one side.

Leo noticed an analytical thoroughness in her actions. She moved slowly, like a scientist conducting an experiment. That was unusual. More often, people move quickly and carelessly when curiosity and grief were involved.

Andreja turned her attention to the notepaper. She picked it up with long, slender fingers, then unfolded it and began to read.

"It's written in Latvian," she said. The emotion had left her voice now. "It's my mother's writing." Her eyes widened and her lips pursed. "You're kidding me," she whispered.

"What does it say?" Allissa asked.

"If you're reading this, then I am no longer with you," Andreja read slowly, pausing to translate the words in the slanted handwriting. "It is no exaggeration to say that the book now in your possession is the reason we are both alive. We would not have made it out in 1973 without it. Then again, without it, maybe your father and Emilija would still be with us. The information in this book has the power for great change. Make sure you use it wisely."

Andreja placed the letter carefully on the table. She looked up at Leo and Allissa, her eyes wide with emotion.

"Is that all it says?" Allissa asked.

Andreja nodded. "My mother never said much."

"Your mother was a spy?" Leo asked.

"Yes." Andreja nodded. Her eyes locked on Leo. "Sort of, anyway. She told people she was a secretary at the University of Latvia. When I got older, I realised what she said didn't make sense. There was no reason a secretary would be rescued like we were and have this new life financed for her. That just didn't make any sense. I knew she must have done something important, or at least known something."

"And that important information is in here." Allissa pointed at the book.

Andreja turned the leather-bound notebook and carefully lifted open the cover. It smelled musty and of decay. Incomprehensible scrawl covered each of the yellowed pages.

"They're a list of names and dates," Andreja said. "Twenty-third of January, 1969. Janis Ozolins came to see Zids. They spoke for several hours. This is the second visit in as many weeks."

"This could be a record of the information she was passing on. That would certainly be valuable," Allissa said. "Do you remember how she communicated the information?"

"Yes, she would send postcards to an address in Paris every few weeks. She told us they were to an old school friend. They must have been written in code, though. But, none of this makes any sense. These records are over fifty years old. How is this going to teach us anything about Emilija?"

"Maybe some of the people mentioned in here are still alive," Leo suggested.

"It's possible." Andreja carefully turned a few pages. "There is information here right up to when we left in 1973."

"We need to go through it and compile a list of all the names we can find. Then we'll try to make contact with them," Allissa said, pulling out a notepad and pen.

"Sure, I guess," Andreja muttered, then sighed. She looked exhausted now. The anger had faded.

"Don't worry," Allissa said, reaching out and putting her hand over Andreja's. "We will find enough to make sure you get the house."

Andreja turned back to the start of the book. "You guys better be as good as Mervin thinks you are."

## 17

Leo stepped outside the cottage and looked up at the sky. The restless afternoon was turning into a balmy summer evening. The sun sank across the distant sea, draining the clear blue into shades of pink and mauve. Across the headland, the water shimmered in the fading light.

He blinked as the fresh air of the evening hit his face and filled his lungs. His head throbbed after several hours of squinting over Marija Panasenko's slanted handwriting and more coffees than he could remember.

"We'll get onto researching these people," Allissa told Andreja. "We'll be in touch in a few days."

Andreja smiled wearily and pushed the door closed.

The buzzing of insects had subsided with the coming dusk, but the chorus of birds had intensified. Leo walked down the path and swung open the gate.

Leo drew the car keys from his pocket and thumbed the button. His newly-purchased 2002 Fiat Panda beeped as it unlocked.

Allissa glanced at the car and smiled.

"What?" Leo said, crossing the road and sliding into the driver's seat. The journey over from Brighton had been their first outing in the car.

"Nothing." Allissa's grin intensified.

"It was a great buy. The guy was virtually giving it away." Leo pushed the key into the ignition and the engine strained to life.

"Oh really," Allissa said, dropping into the passenger seat. "A mean machine like this, I'm surprised he didn't have people queuing around the block."

"It's a good runner, great economy, and —"

"The ugliest car I've ever seen. Why would anyone want a Fiat Panda, especially in gold?" Allissa laughed. "Anyway, we've got a lot to do. No time to worry about your pride and joy. There's no telling what secrets are in that book, but most of them aren't going to be relevant to us. We'll have to stay laser focused on this one."

Leo nodded, glanced over his shoulder, and clicked the lever for the indicator. The windscreen wipers rattled and scraped across the glass. Leo swore and pulled another lever. The radio lit up and a loud hiss bellowed from the speakers. Finally, Leo found the right lever. The indicator flashed and Leo pulled out onto the deserted road.

"Nicely done," Allissa said, laughing. "Are you sure you know what you're doing?"

It was dark by the time they drove into Brighton. The Fiat creaked to a stop at a red light. Leo gazed out across the deserted grass of Victoria Gardens at the warm glow of the King and Queen pub. Two men sat in the window, drinking pints and looking out at the passing traffic. Waiting for the traffic light to change, Leo tried to remember the last time he had been in that pub. Several years ago, at least. He couldn't remember ever visiting with Allissa. Maybe his last visit had been with Mya.

The traffic light blinked to green, but Leo didn't move, too absorbed in his memories. The driver behind him protested with his horn. The sound shook Leo from his reverie. The impatient driver pulled into the outside lane and thundered past them.

True to form, Allissa slept beside him in the passenger seat. She had an enviable ability to sleep on any form of transport. Whereas Leo would sit wide awake for hours on end, Allissa would be straight off to sleep in moments.

Leo pulled to a stop outside their flat a few minutes later. Navigating Brighton's streets in the light evening traffic was easy. Allissa was making a load of fuss over nothing. Owning a car was a great idea. He glanced up at the darkened bay windows on the third floor. A fleeting sense of warmth at the prospect of being home engulfed him. It was nice to be back. It was nice to sleep in the same bed every night, and it was nice not to be in danger at every turn of their work. Leo would be happy if that continued for some months to come.

"We're here," Leo said, shaking Allissa gently. "You get out here. I'll go and find a parking space."

Allissa opened her eyes, yawned, and stretched. "That was quick," she said, twisting her muscles back into use.

"Yep, that's what happens when you fall asleep ten minutes into the journey. Go on, get out, otherwise you can come and hunt for a parking space with me."

"Nope, parking this beast is all on you." Allissa said, glancing at Leo. "I'll get the kettle on. We've got some work to do on this now." Allissa pushed open the door and clambered out. She walked to their front door and turned to see Leo roll away off in search of a parking space.

Allissa stepped into the dark flat and groped around for the light switch. After living in the flat for nearly a year, and spending almost every day of the last six months here, she should know where the bloody light switch was. Running her hand across the rough wallpaper, which she suspected had been in position as long as she'd been on the planet, Allissa found the switch, clicked it on, and the lights blazed to life.

The flat was stiflingly hot, despite the windows being left open.

Allissa padded through to the kitchen and set about making coffee. She was excited that a new case had come up. Six months in one place was more than enough for her. She needed to get out and do something. There were only so many times you could do the same walk down the seafront.

"That wasn't too bad," Leo said, clattering through the door a few minutes later. "I think I've found a good place now." He explained the location on some faraway street.

"That's miles," Allissa said, passing him the coffee. "You'll need to get a taxi from there."

"No, it's not. It's a few minutes' walk. It's fine. And you can park there almost all the time. We just have to make sure we move it by quarter to eight on weekdays."

Allissa took a sip of her coffee in an attempt to hide an eye roll from Leo. As she'd suspected, owning that bloody car was a total waste of time. Although the passenger seat was pretty comfortable.

## 18

Andreja picked up a large glass of red wine and took a deep sip. The glass was already nearly empty. She couldn't believe this was happening to her.

Sure, her mother had been one of the most stubborn and opinionated women she'd ever met, but to force her only daughter on some mad wild goose chase from beyond the grave, that really was the stuff of fiction. Andreja's fingers tightened around the glass. Maybe she should just let Merrowford give the estate to the socialists. Andreja knew she'd be alright. She had her own place, where she used to live, up in London. That was before she'd decided to move down here, to care for her mother in her final years.

She turned to face the kitchen. Most of the space lay in gloom. For almost ten years Andreja had given up her work, her life, to care for her mother. And now, to continue living in the house, her home, she needed to go on some bonkers witch-hunt.

Andreja finished her wine and refilled the glass. She crossed the room and sat down at the table. The leather-bound book lay open in front of her. She and the detectives had spent hours combing through every page of the thing. The truth was, it didn't make any sense. Most of it was information about who had visited who, and when.

"Mr Petersons visited the colonel on the twelfth of March 1971," Andreja read out loud from the page before her.

There were a few names and some addresses, too. Leo and Allissa had taken photographs and were going to see if they could make contact with any. Andreja didn't hold out any hope.

*Whatever secrets were in this book,* she thought as she flipped the pages restlessly, *their meaning died with my mother.*

## 19

"Mr Mikhail," came the voice through the hatch on the unassuming door. "I didn't know we'd see you again, soon to be president and everything."

Mikhail nodded, but didn't say anything. He'd been visiting this backstreet club for years. He wasn't going to let his political ambitions get in the way of that.

A series of bolts clunked and clanged, and the door swung open. The smell of pungent cigarette smoke and alcohol drifted out. The distant sound of music tumbled into the night.

The news of Mikhail's run for presidency had dominated the headlines since his announcement two days earlier. He'd been invited to appear on all the country's major TV and radio stations, which of course he accepted.

As he'd hoped, his announcement had forced three other candidates to prematurely announce their intention to run too. They were already looking like unprepared idiots in comparison to Mikhail. Whilst he wasn't the president yet, he intended to look like it from now on.

"I like this place," Mikhail said, smiling in the gloom. "Even the president needs to relax, right?"

"It's our pleasure to have you," the man said, beckoning Mikhail inside. "Your usual private room?"

Mikhail nodded, then followed the man down the winding mass of staircases and corridors. They passed a door. The muffled sound of pleasurable groans came from within. They turned right and left again. The man pulled open a thick wooden door and beckoned Mikhail inside.

The room was dimly lit and draped in fabrics of red and black. A circular sofa surrounded a glass table.

The man produced a tablet. His fingers darted across the screen, the glow lighting his face. He handed the device to Mikhail. "As you'll see, we have a very fine selection tonight. Of course, discretion is assured."

Mikhail flicked through the photographs, selected one, and passed the tablet back.

"A good choice sir. And the usual to drink?"

Mikhail nodded again.

"I'll have the girls bring it in for you."

Mikhail settled into the sofa. The man closed the door softly. Music streamed from hidden speakers somewhere in the room. The music contained no words, just an ethereal soundscape of instruments. Footsteps clicked down a distant corridor.

Mikhail took a deep breath and let his eyes close for a moment. *This time next month, all going well.*

His thoughts were interrupted by the door clicking open. A pair of women entered. One carried a bottle of scotch, the other a glass. Beneath the heavy make-up, Mikhail assessed them to be early twenties. They both wore the tired expressions of lost innocence. A mixture of excitement and lust welled inside him. *Perfect*, he thought, sitting up and smiling.

One woman poured him a drink, while the other sunk into the sofa beside him.

Mikhail emptied his glass and demanded another. After it had been refilled, he explained his plans for the evening.

"Yes, of course, Mr President," the women said in unison.

## 20

Leo opened his eyes and was dazzled by the early morning summer sun. The curtains were shut, but a bar of bright light pierced through the gap where they didn't quite meet. Leo cursed himself for not replacing them years ago. He stretched, yawned and rolled over, hoping for sleep to come again. He knew it wouldn't. Once Leo was awake, that was it.

Allissa slept soundly beside him. After returning from New York, they hadn't discussed them sharing a room, it just happened. Allissa's clothes were still in the smaller bedroom, but come bedtime they would pad together into Leo's bed.

Leo opened his eyes and watched the rise and fall of her chest. Her long, dark curls spread out on the pillow behind her. A strange sensation of extreme happiness welled through him.

Leo forced himself to sit up. Despite spending more time in the flat in the last six months, he hadn't improved the condition of the place. The bright morning light highlighted the paintwork's multitude of patches and shades. Leo was used to it now, though. Once you got used to something, you hardly even noticed it.

Leo got out of bed, got dressed, and pulled on his faded red trainers. He would go for a run before they got started. He feared the day would involve a lot of time staring at the computer.

"I've just been in touch with the records office in Riga," Allissa said as Leo walked into the front room forty-five minutes later, still panting hard from his run.

"Already?"

"Yeah, it was a funny thing," Allissa said, then grinned and stretched. "I heard an elephant stomping around this morning, so thought I might as well get up and get on with this. I mean, we've got some catching up to do."

"And?"

"Well, I mean we've got some catching up to do because we're nearly fifty years behind already."

"No, I mean what did the person at the records office say?" Leo slumped into a chair and tugged off his trainers.

"The lady I spoke with was actually pretty informative. A lot of the older files, from before independence, are still kept on paper. She was able to find this one really quickly though, and that's where it got very interesting." Allissa paused to finish typing the email.

"Right? What?"

"Well..." Allissa cleared her throat and put the laptop on the coffee table. "Emilija Panasenko doesn't exist."

"Do you mean she doesn't exist because she's dead?"

"No, she never existed, according to the records." Allissa leaned back onto the sofa and folded her arms.

"But we know she existed. She was, or is, Andreja's sister."

"Yes, but that's the thing. There is no record of her at all.

No birth, no death, no bank accounts, no passport, nothing. It's like she didn't exist at all. She's a ghost."

Leo's gaze narrowed. "How's that even possible? We know her date of birth, her place of birth. Surely they have something."

"The lady explained that it's actually more common than you'd think in former Eastern Bloc countries. Because of the changes in power, some records were never kept, and others are missing."

"Information is power," Leo said, frowning.

"Exactly," Allissa replied.

"The next thing," Allissa said, passing a sheet of paper across to Leo, "is to go through the contacts that Marija left in the book. I'd expect most of them to be dead ends after all these years."

Leo nodded. "It's worth a try, though. You never know what might turn up. I'll take the first half."

"Sure." Allissa highlighted several names and settled back into the sofa.

"How are you getting on?" Leo asked, coming back into the front room with two steaming mugs of coffee. They'd spent several hours searching for the names listed in the back of Marija's notebook, but had found scant information about any of them.

"Not great. Thanks," Allissa said, accepting the coffee. "All the results were either the wrong age, dead, or in no way connected with Riga. I found obituaries for two of them. I've printed them just to be thorough. Then for one guy I found absolutely nothing. He's a ghost. There's no one in the world called Evvas Kenneit, apparently."

"Well, that's not true. I went to school with a guy called Evvas Kenneit." Leo took a sip of his coffee. "He was a great guy."

"Really?"

"No, of course not." Leo giggled.

"What about you?"

"Pretty much the same. Nothing useful. One obituary. Two ghosts, and one... well, check this out." Leo grabbed a sheet of paper from the printer and passed it to Allissa.

The page was a printout of a business directory.

"Valdis Jansons Locksmiths," Allissa read out loud. "No way. This can't be him. If he was involved with Marija back in the seventies, he must now be —"

"Seventy or eighty something. You're right, but look at that." Leo pointed further down the page where customers had left reviews. Valdis Jansons Locksmiths had three reviews. "Look at the third one. The computer translated it for me.

Allissa read it out loud.

"I'm not sure what this guy was doing. I asked for one copy of the key and he changed the locks on the entire apartment. Charged me damn nearly 150€. I would have refused to pay if he hadn't been so old." She glanced at Leo. "It could be him," Allissa said, grabbing her phone and dialling the number printed at the top of the page.

Leo shuffled onto the sofa beside her.

Allissa switched to the speakerphone as the ringing tone buzzed.

"Come on," Leo muttered, eyes fixed on the phone.

The phone continued to ring.

Allissa glanced from Leo back to the phone on the coffee table.

Suddenly there was a clunk on the line. Something buzzed.

Leo's eyes widened.

"Ja," came a thickly-accented voice.

Leo and Allissa looked at each other, their eyes alight with excitement.

"Ja," the voice came again, louder this time. Something clunked and buzzed.

"Hello," Allissa said slowly. "Do you speak English?"

There was no reply. The sound of the buzzing swelled and then died.

"Yes," the voice came again. It was thick and gruff. "Who this?"

"My name's Allissa Stockwell, and I'm looking to speak with Valdis Jansons."

The buzz came back. It sounded like a freight train changing tracks.

"I am Valdis Jansons. Locksmith. You need locksmith?"

"No, I don't need a locksmith." Allissa considered the best way to approach the next question. "I'm looking for information about a woman called Emilija Panasenko. Her mother, Marija Panasenko, suggested we speak with someone called Valdis Jansons. Is that you?"

Silence. The freight train rattled some more.

"Say again," Jansons said.

*Was that surprise in the man's voice?* Allissa wondered. She simplified the question and tried again.

"Do you know anyone called Emilija Panasenko or Marija Panasenko?"

No reply came. The line went quiet. Steel clattered against steel.

Neither Leo nor Allissa dared to look away from the phone as though they might miss the answer.

The, the line went dead. It was as though the chord had been cut with a pair of scissors. Allissa's phone faded to black.

## 21

Valdis Jansons' pale eyes narrowed when he heard a name that time should have forgotten. Suddenly he was alert. He pushed the thick plastic handset tighter against his ear. His eyes roamed his apartment. Nothing looked unusual. The late morning light cast an angular shadow through his thin curtains and across the threadbare brown carpet.

Could this be some kind of joke? Could someone be tricking him?

His grey lips made the movement of speech without any sound coming forth. He'd suddenly forgotten the English words. The language felt strange.

There was a rumble and a clatter down the line.

"Do you know anyone called Emilija Panasenko or Marija Panasenko?"

The voice came again, faint but definite. Jansons had definitely heard it. He tried to hone in on the voice to memorise it like he would a face. It sounded English — proper English, not just someone speaking English.

He listened closely to the electronic buzz of his old telephone. His heart juddered and adrenaline raced. Something clanged somewhere in the phone system. Jansons thought of chains falling down concrete government stairwells. He cursed these modern systems. They didn't make them like they used to. Things were different now, but he still had to be careful. If he ever planned on finding out the truth, he still had to look over his shoulder. Jansons had been looking over his shoulder his whole life. He wasn't going to stop now. He couldn't stop now.

Jansons' nicotine-stained fingers snatched up a paper and pen from between the locks in various stages of disrepair on the table. He glared at the phone's tiny digital screen, which displayed the caller's number. The system had been cutting-edge when Jansons had got it. He'd paid a lot of money for it, too. Made in China. None of this East German rubbish. He needed a decent system so that he could see who was calling. Although, that was all very well when he could find his wretched glasses. The digits now swam in front of his eyes.

Jansons tapped frantically at the pockets of his trousers and jacket. Nowhere. He glanced around the room. Distances had never bothered him. It was up close that things were trouble. He could make out a car registration number from fifty paces, but couldn't even see the number on a euro note without his glasses. But then again, who wanted euro notes anyway?

There! They were on the arm of the sofa next to his cigarettes and the ashtray. A tendril of smoke snaked upwards from the cigarette he'd left burning when he'd got up to answer the phone.

Jansons darted across the room, his phone still in his hand. The long, coiled cable dragged across the floor. He knew he should get one of those new mobile phones. They were all the rage now. None of these wires, or anything like that. It seemed complicated. There was safety in simplicity. That's what Jansons always used to say, and he still believed it now.

He slid the glasses over his nose and crossed back to the phone's cradle. He examined the screen now and noted down the number. He could tell from the digits that it was an English mobile phone. Faint noises fizzed down the line. The speaker was still there. Jansons couldn't speak now. Not like this. He had been careful for too long to risk this now. He hung up.

His breathing suddenly sounded loud in the empty room. His pulse raced.

Marija Panasenko. Someone had spoken with Marija Panasenko. Jansons needed to speak with them, that he knew for sure. With what Marija knew when she disappeared, this could at last be a breakthrough.

## 22

Leo and Allissa looked at each other, and then back at the phone.

"What happened there?" Leo asked.

"I... uh, I'm not sure." Allissa picked up the phone. It glowed. "It looked fine. The call must have disconnected. Not sure why."

"Strange," Leo said, looking at the printed profile for Jansons Locksmiths. "It was a long shot, anyway. But —"

"There was something unusual though, wasn't there?" Allissa interrupted. "The way he hesitated when I said the names. It sounded as though he recognised them and was thinking about how best to respond."

"Maybe. Or maybe he didn't really speak English and didn't know what you were on about." Leo laid the paper down on the coffee table.

"Do we have anything else to go on?"

"Nope," Leo said, exhaling. "A bunch of names of people that by all accounts never existed. How is that even possible?"

Allissa shook her head. "It's worth another try, then."

She unlocked her phone, redialled the long Latvian number, and tapped the speakerphone button.

The call connected and rang. The stark electronic buzz of the ringing tone sounded. Neither Leo nor Allissa spoke. Both imagined the trill ringing of the telephone in an apartment somewhere in Riga.

## 23

Jansons hurried past the lift — *out of order* — and took the steps as quickly as he could. The lift hadn't worked for many years. In fact, Jansons had lived here for approaching sixty years and only remembered using the stupid thing a handful of times. The stairwell reeked of damp. Fortunately, he lived on the first floor, so didn't have far to go. Someone on the floor below him was cooking. The smell was unfamiliar to Jansons. Everything was different now, even the smell of the food.

Jansons hustled through the door and out into the bright morning sun. He squinted up at the cloudless sky. The sun warmed his face. Maybe this was the Europe-wide heatwave everyone had been talking about. The hottest in a long time, apparently.

Jansons pushed his hat down low to shade his eyes and scampered off towards the train station. He paused at the crossing as the passenger train to Riga rumbled past. The blue and yellow livery of the ancient machine glowed hopefully in the sun.

He crossed the railway and paused. He could see the

phone box from here. He needed to be cautious, though. It always paid to be cautious. Jansons positioned himself on a bench and fished the packet of cigarettes from his pocket. He slid one out and lit it with a steady hand that belied his age. Jansons smoked and watched people coming and going from the train station and the small shop on the other side of the tracks. That was one good thing with being old; you were allowed to sit and rest. A younger man watching the comings and goings of his neighbours might be noticed, but Jansons blended into the scenery. Jansons lit another cigarette with the butt of the last. The next train rumbled into the station, this one going in the direction of Pazazieru. Families with children going for a day at the beach perhaps. Those people didn't concern Jansons. He was looking for something else. Some sign that he was being followed or watched. He saw nothing. Jansons stubbed out his second cigarette and ground it into the dust with the heel of his shoe.

He'd waited long enough. He climbed to his feet and crossed to the phone box. Curiosity cursed through him. He wanted to know what the mystery caller knew about Marija Panasenko.

## 24

"That's strange, right?" Allissa said. "Why would he answer the first time, but not now?"

"Maybe he blocked your number."

"Yes, but why? The only reason he would have to block my number is if the names meant something to him." Allissa tapped the phone against her chin.

Leo nodded.

"Have we got an address?"

Leo scooted back over to his computer and tapped a few keys. "Yeah. He lives in an apartment building in Zolitūde, Riga."

"Interesting." Allissa looked from her phone to Leo. Leo caught her eye.

"I know exactly what you're thinking," Leo said. "We can't go all the way there just because a guy hung up on us. As I said, he may just not have understood what you were saying. The guy might be deaf for all you know."

"Then why wouldn't he answer when we called back?" Allissa asked, her eyes shining with excitement.

"I... well, maybe he just went out." Leo's conviction didn't make it as far as his expression.

"Look, we've got a duty to find out all we can, right?"

"Yes, of course."

"We've pretty much exhausted all the options we can on the phone and by looking online. What else can we do?"

"We could... urm... go over these names again." Leo spun around in his chair and examined the list of names on the screen.

"Sure, okay, well do that. But when that comes up with nothing, as it will because we've already tried, then we're going to Riga."

Leo's throat was suddenly dry. He glanced beyond his computer and out of the bay window. The slates of Brighton's rooftops were silhouetted against the sliver surface of the sea. Their previous cases, in which they'd had to visit dark and sinister places, slipped through his mind. The killers in Kathmandu; burned alive in Hong Kong; threatened by gangs in Berlin; and just a few months ago, entangled in the deranged plans of a serial killer in New York.

"But... b-but..." Leo stuttered, anxiety welling in his chest. "We've... we've got our system now. We can send the work on to someone there. They know the place, know what they're dealing with —"

"And that means we don't have to go anywhere," Allissa interrupted.

"No, it's not, uh, it's not that," Leo managed.

Allissa slid her phone down to the coffee table and crossed the room towards Leo. She put her arms around him and nestled her face beside his. "Yes, we've done some dangerous things, but we've always got out alive."

"Only just." The image of Allissa in the clutches of the serial killer swam through Leo's mind.

"Only just is good enough for me," Allissa said. "You've come so far since we met. There's no way I'm letting you slip back into spending your whole life in this flat. There's a whole world out there and I'm not paying someone else to experience it for me."

Leo put his arms over Allissa's and took control of his breathing. His anxiety was part of him, it always would be, but it didn't control him. Anxiety might be along for the ride, but Leo couldn't let it anywhere near the driving seat.

"Sure, yeah, I know." Leo turned and kissed Allissa on the cheek. His anxiety faded and a new feeling welled inside him. One that was as strong, but different.

The phone on the coffee table behind them trilled. Allissa straightened up and crossed the room. Leo instantly missed her close to him.

Allissa picked up the phone and turned to face him. Her face lit up with excitement.

"It's a Latvian number," she said.

## 25

Jansons pushed the thick plastic handset of the payphone against his ear. He turned and scrutinised the scene behind him. Nothing looked unusual. A man in dark clothes walked a dog and smoked a cigarette. The man paused beside a lamppost for the dog to mark its territory and then wandered aimlessly in the direction of the train station.

"Come on, come on," Jansons muttered as the phone rang. He suddenly felt very exposed. He should have gone to a call box further from his apartment. What was he thinking? How could he have been so stupid? This is how people got caught. He was about to hang up when the line clicked and a voice spoke.

"Hello." The voice was crystal clear in comparison to the noise on the line in his apartment. It was the same woman as before. That was proof Jansons' phone was tapped. It certainly had nothing to do with his forty-year-old phone.

"Hello," Jansons whispered, his eyes making another circuit of his surroundings. "You called me. You want to talk about Marija Panasenko?"

. . .

"It's him," Allissa mouthed, "Jansons."

Leo grabbed a notepad and a pen, and sat beside Allissa. Allissa activated the speaker and put her phone on the coffee table.

"Yes," Allissa said. "Let me explain. We are missing persons' investigators and we're looking for Marija Panasenko's daughter, Emilija."

"You working for Marija?" Jansons spoke in short bursts. It sounded as though he was nervous.

"Yes, sort of," Allissa said. "I'm sorry to tell you that Marija died a few weeks ago. One of her dying wishes was to know what happened to her daughter, Emilija."

"Marija is dead? Did they get her?"

Allissa explained that Marija had been ill for some time and that her death was of natural causes. Jansons listened intently.

"I'm sorry to have to tell you that. Were you close?"

"Yes, many years. A lifetime ago, in fact. We have had no contact since she moved to England. That was decided. It was not safe to contact."

"We're now looking for information about Marija's daughter, Emilija. We've already spoken to someone from the public records department and there seems to be no record of her at all. Would you be able to help us?"

"Her daughter, Emilija, was caught during the escape, yes?"

"That's what we understand, yes."

"They would have given her a new identity. Forced her to use it. All record of her previous identity would have been destroyed."

"Okay," Allissa said. Leo made a note of that. "How can we find out what her new identity was?"

"Ah, now that's a big problem," Jansons explained,

warming to his theme. "When we got independence from Soviet Union all records were taken."

"What do you mean, taken?"

"I mean, not there. Stolen. All criminal records, records of people involved in KGB, records of births, deaths... we have nothing. All gone. There are many rumours that they are hidden somewhere in our country. Believe it or not, there are still people loyal to the old ways, even after all this time. But the thing is, those records would be, how you say, explosive. Very bad for some very important people."

"Why?" Allissa asked.

"Everything they did before 1993 was in those records. Maybe thief, maybe informant, maybe killer, whatever. In 1993 they got a new chance when the records were gone."

"And that's where Emilija's new identity would be."

"I suppose so, yes. I have been looking for many years. Now I am old man and have no idea." Jansons coughed violently for a few seconds. "If those files come out, is much more important than the name of Marija's daughter. They would bring down the government."

## 26

Andreja woke with her head thumping. She was tangled in the sheets and had vague memories of relentless dreams, none of which were as strange or harrowing as her current reality. She rubbed a hand across her face and blinked. Her fingers came away damp. She took a deep breath and grumbled. The day looked bright behind the thick floral curtains. She tried to move her legs, but they felt heavy. She glanced down to see Tommy, her mother's ginger cat. In a strange mix of genetics, laziness and overeating, Tommy had grown to twice the size a cat should be. Andreja twisted and pulled her legs out from beneath the chunky animal. Tommy opened one eye, glared at her, and then settled back down to sleep some more.

"It's alright for you," Andreja snarled, fighting her way out of bed. "You don't have to deal with this rubbish."

Andreja entered the kitchen and saw two empty wine bottles standing to attention on the draining board. She groaned and ran a hand down across her hair. A half empty glass of wine stood on the table beside the notebook. It was a small mercy to learn she hadn't finished that glass too.

Andreja put the kettle on, then poured herself a glass of water and fetched two painkillers. She swallowed them quickly before completing a circuit of the kitchen, pulling the curtains wide and opening the windows. Armed with a steaming mug of coffee, she swung open the patio doors and stepped outside.

She glanced up at the sky and squinted. The sun was yet to reach its zenith, but already the heat was unbearable. Insects busied themselves around the garden's chaotic collection of flowers. The lawn's grass was so long now that it was crisscrossed with the tracks of scurrying nocturnal animals.

Andreja slumped into a garden chair and took the first sip of her coffee. Today would be better than yesterday. It had to be. It couldn't be any worse, that was for sure.

Behind her, somewhere inside the house, her phone rang.

"Here we go. What now?" Andreja muttered. She sat still for a few seconds and considered letting it ring out. She just wanted to be left alone for one day. One day to let herself come to terms with everything that had happened.

The ringing continued.

"Alright, alright," Andreja said, forcing herself to her feet. Her head protested at the movement. She placed a hand against her forehead and closed her eyes.

Andreja stepped back inside and looked around the kitchen for her phone. It glowed from the table beside the mysterious notebook and the glass of wine. That was obviously where she'd left it last night. Andreja grabbed up the phone and thumbed the answer button.

"Andreja, it's Allissa," came the voice down the line.

Andreja muttered a greeting. Her voice was thick and croaky.

"Are you okay? You don't sound very well," Allissa said.

"Yes, yes, fine. How are you getting on?" Andreja slumped down into the chair.

"Yes, it's been an interesting day," Allissa said, telling Andreja of their progress so far.

"Let me get this right. This guy has spent the last thirty years looking for these files, and hasn't found them?"

"That's right. He seemed to think that your mum might have known the place they had planned to take them. Apparently, they had a strategy for keeping the public records in case of liberation from the very beginning. Your mother may not have realised what it was at the time."

"She didn't say anything to me, and we went through that book page by page. There was nothing there." Andreja exhaled and rubbed her eyes.

"No, that's true," Allissa said. "Well, we're continuing to work on it. I'll give you a call back when we have some news."

Andreja hung up without saying goodbye and dropped the phone to the table.

Andreja put her head in her hands and rubbed her eyes again. "This guy has spent thirty years looking. If I don't find anything in one year, I'll lose the house!" Her voice echoed fitfully around the empty kitchen.

What happened next appeared to occur in slow motion.

Andreja dropped her hands down on the table. Her right arm fell, clipping the edge of the wineglass. The glass toppled, first one way and then the other. It moved on its axis as though deciding whether to fall or remain standing. Andreja inhaled. Her eyes sprung wide. The notebook lay open beside the glass.

Andreja made a grab for the rocking glass. It teetered on its precipice. The dark red liquid danced. Andreja tried to grab it. All she succeeded in doing was helping the thing on its way. The glass tipped, as if in slow motion. The red wine sloshed out across the table and onto the open notebook.

Andreja swore again and shot to her feet. The chair fell backwards, clattering to the tiles. The empty glass rolled to the floor and shattered. Andreja grabbed a towel from the kitchen and sprinted back to the table. She dabbed the notebook with the towel, but the wine had already absorbed into the page. Then Andreja noticed something. Her jaw hung loose. She dropped the towel to the floor. On the page of the notebook, beneath her mother's meaningless scrawls, something else appeared. A pattern. A message.

No, it wasn't either of those things. It was a map.

## 27

Jansons paused at the door of his apartment block and surveyed the scene behind him. Four other blocks, constructed in the same grey concrete as his, surrounded a small lawn. Beyond that, pine trees jostled for space and the trains clanged and rattled on the twin tracks from Riga to Jūrmala and back again. The sun was high now and the sky a deep blue.

Jansons squinted and cupped a hand above his eyes. He scanned the square. A man and a woman walked out from the door behind him. The door banged closed. Both were reading something on their phones. Jansons recognised them and greeted them curtly by name.

A man crossed the square in the distance, headphones plugged into his ears.

Everything looked as it should. Jansons didn't think anyone had followed him. An old man using a pay phone? What was wrong with that?

Arriving back at his apartment, Jansons clicked on the radio — a Selga 7 model with the original transistors — and settled at the table. He had told the owner of the nearby shop that he would have his lock ready by the time they closed for business this afternoon. But, try as he might, he just couldn't get the thing to stop sticking. He'd stripped it back, oiled each component, put it back together, but still it wouldn't work smoothly.

As much as Jansons hated to admit defeat, perhaps they would have to buy a new one.

Jansons glanced up at the radio as the signal faded and the thing hissed violently.

Replacing something went against everything Jansons believed in. What was the world's current obsession with shiny and new? It seemed to Jansons as though everyone was trying to forget where they came from. They were so distracted with their little pocket computers and mobile thingy-ma-whats, that they forgot the struggles of old. The Soviet Union was no more, but now people were under the control of another dictator — Wi-Fi signals and tech companies.

Jansons shook his head in an attempt to concentrate. He picked up the lock and examined it. He really should get it fixed. He *would* get it fixed.

## 28

Leo's Fiat Panda crunched to a stop outside Andreja's cottage. He killed the engine. The journey from Brighton had been quicker this time. Despite Leo's circuitous route and twice being stuck in the wake of crawling farm machinery, they had made it in less than two hours. Leo sat back in the driver's seat and mentally scored up a point for car ownership against using public transport.

He unclipped his seatbelt and opened the door. The car slipped slowly forwards. Leo looked around in panic.

In the passenger seat, Allissa pulled up the handbrake and giggled.

"I'm just saying, if we'd got the train here, it would have taken us ages," Leo said, climbing out of the car. "We'd have needed a taxi to Brighton station, it's a route of about a dozen different trains, then another taxi to get here. It's just not practical."

"It may have taken a little longer, yes," Allissa agreed, turning to warm her face in the strong sunshine. "But where's the hurry all of a sudden? This is what I don't understand. The big argument for cars is that they save people time, right?"

"Exactly,"

"Yet, I read the other day that in the last fifty years people spend less time with their families, less time learning new skills, less time outdoors or doing things they enjoy. What are they doing with all this time they're saving? Where's it going?"

Leo shrugged.

"I'd agree, if having a car doubled the number of concert pianists, poets and painters." Allissa opened the gate, and Leo followed her up the path towards the front door. A fat ginger cat examined them from an upstairs window. "But it's just another thing that you'll have to maintain. Plus, you'll have that great game of 'find the parking space' later."

Allissa knocked on the door. The cat scrutinised them closely, considering permission for their entry. The bougainvillea zinged with insects.

"It's fine. I've found a really good parking place now. And it's no more than fifteen minutes' walk away. Twenty max."

Allissa turned and smiled at Leo as the lock clicked and the door swung open. Andreja stood in the doorway. Her face was pale, and her hair hung limp and lifeless. Although she had appeared tired and under pressure the day before, now she looked plain awful.

"Hi. We came as soon as we could. You said you had something important to show us?" Allissa said.

"Yes, yes," Andreja said, beckoning the investigators inside. "It's... it's... um, I didn't know how to explain it on the phone. It's probably just better that you see for yourselves. Leave your shoes on. You'll see why."

Leo and Allissa followed Andreja into the gloomy hallway. Allissa turned and shot Leo a glance of concern.

Neither could guess what Andreja had found that had caused her such upset.

Allissa looked around the kitchen. It was a mess. She noticed the empty wine bottles and assumed they were partly to blame for Andreja's appearance.

A shard of broken glass crunched beneath Allissa's shoe. "What happened?"

Andreja indicated the table, the surface of which was now stained dark red.

"Wine, I assume?" Leo said.

"I've left everything just as it was. I didn't know what to do about —" Andreja pointed at the notebook, which lay open on the table. "I was just clearing up this morning, and I knocked that glass over. It went all over the —" Andreja inhaled deeply and fanned her eyes with her fingers.

"It's okay," Allissa said, laying a comforting hand on her shoulder. "It was lucky we got all we needed from it yesterday. I'm sure the stain won't affect anything."

"No, you don't understand," Andreja said. "Just look, just look."

Leo and Allissa stepped around the table and looked at the notebook. More glass cracked beneath their feet. Leo pulled the notebook towards them on the table. It started to make sense. Wine had soaked into the open pages, covering Marija's scrawls but leaving an outline, or some markings, or a —

"It's a map," Leo declared, looking at Andreja. "Or at least that's what I think it is. It doesn't make a lot of sense though." Leo gently prodded the page. It was almost dry now.

Allissa looked from Leo to the book and then up at Andreja. She was struck by a shard of realisation. "It couldn't be, could it?" She pulled the notebook towards her and then looked up at Leo. "It couldn't be. That would be —"

"I reckon that's exactly what it is," Leo said. "Why would Marija have gone to those lengths to write it in some kind of invisible ink and hide it in a solicitor's safe if it wasn't that important?"

"What's... what do you think it is? What's going on?" Andreja said.

Allissa nodded, the importance of this map blossoming in her mind. "Jansons said that this could take down the government."

Leo and Allissa exchanged a wide-eyed stare.

"Can we trust him, do you think?" Leo said. "I mean, he could be anyone."

"I don't think Marija would have left his name in here if she didn't want us to trust him," Allissa said.

"Hey, what? What's going on?" Andreja repeated.

"What do we do?" Leo said.

"We've got to tell him, haven't we?" Allissa said. "That's the only way he can help —"

"What the hell is going on?" Andreja shouted. Leo and Allissa looked at her.

Allissa straightened up and described the conversation they'd had with Jansons.

"And you think this could be it?"

Leo and Allissa nodded.

"Wow," Andreja said, leaning back onto the kitchen counter. "This could take down the government."

## 29

"But the things is," Allissa said, spinning the notebook around on the table, "I just can't seem to make any sense of it. I mean, how is anyone supposed to know where this is?"

"Jansons might," Leo said, sweeping the broken glass into a pile.

"Maybe but I don't see how, it's just a tiny bit of —"

"What about the other pages?" Andreja crossed the room and flipped over to the next page of the book. "I only spilled this on one page, but the map could be in parts all the way through the book."

"I thought of that," Allissa said, "but to find out, we're going to have to destroy it."

Leo tipped the broken glass in the bin and crossed to the table. "What about if we photograph each page before, in case we need them." Leo and Allissa looked at Andreja.

She considered for a moment. "I guess we have to," she said, her lips forming into her first smile of the day.

The next two hours passed in a blur. Allissa carefully unpicked the notebook's binding so that the pages were loose. Leo took photos of each one, ensuring that the writing was legible, before Allissa and Andreja soaked them in red wine using an old, but thoroughly cleaned, cat litter tray.

As the pages hung on the washing line to dry, Andreja carried cold drinks out onto the patio.

Allissa leaned back and watched a small aeroplane skip through the sky of boundless blue.

"It's a beautiful garden," she said, taking a glass from the tray.

"Yes," Andreja agreed, "my mother loved it. She wanted things to be a bit wild, as you can see. She was all about the insects and animals. Personally, I prefer it a bit more ordered, but she had her ways."

"It's lovely," Leo said, taking a biscuit and snapping it in half. A seagull swung down, perched on the fence, and eyed him with spite.

The papers dried quickly in the warm afternoon. Leo moved the garden furniture aside, swept the patio, and Allissa laid the papers out on the slabs. When they were spread out, Allissa, Leo and Andreja stood back and tried to make sense of the markings.

"It's definitely some kind of map," Allissa said, leaning down and following the route of a road with her finger. "But without knowing what it's of, we can't know if they're in the right positions."

"Maybe it's not even supposed to be set up that way. It might be several maps," Leo said.

Andreja fetched an old Latvian road map and leafed through the pages.

"1993," Leo said, reading the year on the cover.

"Yes, I got this while I was there finishing my degree. It

was just after independence. I wanted to go back and see what the place was like, you know?"

Allissa nodded. She felt the same about visiting her mother's homeland of Kenya. It was something that had lurked at the peripheries of her consciousness for many years. One day soon, she would go. "Did your mother go with you?"

"No." Andreja became suddenly solemn. "She was still worried that it wouldn't be safe. I tried to convince her, but as you already know, my mother could never be persuaded."

Leo, Allissa and Andreja leafed through the map and checked every page against those of the notebook. Nothing.

"I think we're going to need to get some help with this," Leo said as they collected the pages up and put them in a folder. "We're getting nowhere."

"We need to ask Jansons," Allissa said.

Leo reluctantly agreed.

## 30

Jansons' house-phone rang again shortly after he'd returned from reinstalling the locks. Breathing new life into the old system buoyed his mood.

"Ja," Jansons barked, holding the old handset to his ear.

"Mr Jansons, it's Allissa, we spoke earlier."

Jansons was once again suddenly alert. His eyes flicked left and right, then he hung up the phone.

The sun was labouring behind an electricity pylon as Jansons made his way back to the phone box. Shadows crept insidiously across the square like great fingers, and gloom clung to the underside of the pine trees. The streetlights clicked on as he approached the rail crossing. The train to Jūrmala was due at any moment. Jansons hurried to get across the track before the train arrived.

Nearing the phone box, he slowed and went through the same routine of looking around.

When he was satisfied that no one was looking, he grabbed the handset and dialled the number. A train rumbled into the station behind him. The locomotive's bright headlights washed the trees in an unearthly glow. Jansons turned to watch a crowd of people pile out onto the platform.

"Hello," came the woman's voice down the impossibly clear line. "Is that you?"

"Yes. Now tell me, what have you found?"

Jansons pressed the phone to his ear and listened intently for the next few minutes. His pulse raced as the woman explained about the map they were struggling to make sense of. Jansons was acutely aware — although he refused to concede to it yet — that this may be the news he had been seeking for almost fifty years.

Was it even possible that Marija knew the location of the secret file store? Jansons' mind tumbled through possible solutions and theories. She had associated with some pretty well-informed people back then, most of whom underestimated her as the secretary she appeared to be. Very few people had come to the same realisation as Jansons — Marija Panasenko was a force to be reckoned with, both in intelligence and spirit.

"Mr Jansons, are you there?" the woman said, interrupting his thoughts.

"Yes, yes."

"Well?"

"Well, what?"

"Is there any way we can send you a digital photograph of these images? It would be great to see if you can make any sense of it."

"No, I don't think so. I don't see how that's possible."

"Do you know anyone who has a smartphone or a computer you could use? This really would be helpful to us."

Jansons was losing patience now. Did this woman not

understand? These were documents of the most secret nature. They couldn't just be sent to the internet and viewed on a borrowed computer.

"I'm sorry, no. And I tell you, do not put these images anywhere on the internet. They must stay secure."

"I know. I can assure you we'll take care of them. We could just do with your help to try and make sense of them. Are you sure there's no way?"

"No," Jansons roared. "I can't help you like this. I'm putting myself in great danger already. If you want me to help you, you'll have to come and show me." Jansons slammed down the phone and turned. The sun had disappeared now, and darkness enclosed him on all sides. Despite the mildness of the evening, Jansons turned up the collar of his jacket and hurried in the direction of home.

## 31

Allissa hung up the phone and looked first at Andreja, and then at Leo.

The outside light had faded, but the patio doors remained open. A light breeze drifted into the kitchen.

"We're going to have to go to Riga," Leo said slowly. He caught Allissa's eye. The shadow of anxiety rushed through him. He had got so comfortable spending the last few months in Brighton, that the idea of going elsewhere now was alien and unwelcome.

Andreja walked to the fridge and pulled out a bottle of white wine. "I'm coming too," she said, pouring herself a glass. She offered one to the others. Allissa accepted, but Leo shook his head.

"You really don't need to do that," Allissa said. "You've got a lot to do here, with the house and all that stuff. Your mother contracted us to do this, so you don't need to feel —"

"You speak Latvian, do you?" Andreja said. Her eyes held a challenge.

"No, but —"

"Then you'll need me. I'm more involved in this than you are. It's final, no discussion."

Allissa glanced at Leo, who nodded almost imperceptibly.

"Okay," Allissa said, pulling out her laptop. "Let's see how soon we can get there."

## 32

Leo glanced through the window of the Baltic Air flight as they banked across the Gulf of Riga. Two days had passed since the discovery of the map in Andreja's cottage and, as ever, things had moved quickly.

As usual, Allissa charged herself with arranging the logistics of the trip. She'd booked two rooms in a hotel in central Riga, one for Andreja, and for the first time, a double bed for her and Leo. Leo glanced at her sleeping in the seat beside him, her eyes shut tight against the fierce sun which was just sinking beyond a nebulous horizon. Normally this part of an investigation brought with it a thread of anxiety, which Leo's overactive mind couldn't help but tug on until it all unravelled in a great mess of worry. This time, thought Leo as the delicate spires of Riga's churches came into view beside the wide, quicksilver smudge of the Daugava River, things were different. Something — somehow — felt better this time.

Leo looked at Allissa again; a picture of tranquillity in an oversized jumper, her hair tied up beneath a bright headscarf.

Allissa wasn't the reason he felt okay, though, Leo assured himself. No. He felt positive about this case for several reasons. He furrowed his brow and counted the reasons out on his fingers. Number one, they were pretty experienced at finding missing people now. To start with, back in the dangerous, dark days of Kathmandu, Leo didn't know anything about finding missing people. Now, their clients treated them like experts. Number two, this was a European city, just a few hundred miles from home. English would probably be widely spoken here. It wasn't a far-flung and distant corner of the globe. Number three, this case had been cold for nearly fifty years. The chance of them upsetting someone by investigating a disappearance that happened all that time ago was unlikely. Leo hoped for that, anyway. Number four... He looked at Allissa. His scowl of concentration melted into a smile. He forced himself to concentrate again. Number four, he and Allissa were now... He and Allissa were now... used to working with each other. That felt good, too. Leo put his hand over Allissa's and rested his head on hers.

Where normally his anxiety of the unknown prowled, snapping beneath the surface, another feeling simmered. It was an emotion that he hadn't accepted yet, but one he knew all too well. Leo closed his eyes.

Leo's eyes shot open. The plane bounced and shook. He looked around, disorientated and confused.

"We've just landed," Allissa said, yawning and stretching. "How long were you asleep for?"

"I wasn't asleep, I think."

"You were snoring thirty seconds ago."

Leo looked out of the window. The plane rumbled along the tarmac towards the terminal. Darkness obscured most of the airport, but spears of pink still highlighted the sky.

"About a minute," he said. "Bloody typical."

"This way," Allissa said, leading them in the direction of the passport control a few minutes later. The movement, and the fresh evening air as they'd climbed down the stairs from the plane, shook Leo back into reality.

They reached the passport control area and joined the queue which Allissa assessed to be the shortest. Typically, as it turned out, all the other queues moved at twice the speed of theirs. Leo glanced at the immigration officer at the front of their queue. A woman in her fifties scrutinised each passport with incredible care.

Leo glanced across at Andreja in the queue to their left. She had sat in the row in front of them on the plane and they hadn't spoken yet.

Leo felt uneasy about sharing their investigation with someone else. Sure, he and Allissa had needed people in the past to translate, or help them with local knowledge, but to Andreja this was personal. A knot of doubt turned in Leo's mind. Leo examined it as the line shuffled forwards. Sure, Andreja knew the city and the situation, but she was also emotionally involved. Leo knew too well that things became difficult when emotions were involved.

Andreja reached the front of the line, stepped forward, and handed her passport to the immigration officer.

Watching her, Leo reasoned that they had no choice. Andreja, in a way, was the client. She wanted to come with them, so they couldn't stop her. They were stuck with her. She was paying for the investigation in a way. Or at least, her mother was.

Leo watched the immigration officer examine Andreja. He studied her passport, then looked at the screen of his computer. The officer scrutinised the passport closely a second time. Long seconds passed. The officer placed the passport on the scanner. Finally, as though making a decision, he snapped the passport shut, slid it back across the desk and signalled for Andreja to pass. His eyes followed her as she walked through into the arrival's hall.

"Come on, move forward." Allissa poked Leo in the ribs.

"Sorry, yes," Leo said, stepping forward.

Passport checks always made Leo nervous. He couldn't really explain why. He supposed it was the thought that someone had the ability to deny your entry to their country, or maybe, at the touch of a button, call men with guns to escort you away. As with many of Leo's anxieties, he knew it had no basis in fact.

Fifteen minutes later, Andreja, Allissa and Leo piled into a taxi. Andreja instructed the driver in quick-fire Latvian to take them to central Riga. Leo shuddered in the aggressive cool of the taxi's air conditioning. It seemed Riga was experiencing the same restless heat as they had in Brighton.

The outskirts of the city, shrouded in night, scrolled past the taxi. After twenty minutes, the taxi paused at a traffic light and an ancient blue and white tram rattled past. The tram was all but empty except for a grey-haired woman on the back seat who stared morosely out at the waiting cars. The lights of the oncoming cars streaked across the tarmac.

The traffic light flicked from red to green. The taxi set off and swung to the left. Leo peered out at a large triangular glass building. Still following the tram, they crossed the wide expanse of the Daugava River. The lights of the city danced tantalisingly in the inky water.

The taxi made a few sharp turns down the increasingly small and picturesque streets of central Riga and drew up outside a brightly-lit building. Rows of ornate balconies jutted from its facade. The roof was crowned with domes and spires.

"We're here," Allissa said, scrambling out of the taxi. Leo gazed up at the vast building. The opulent light of the reception area shone out through the glass of the revolving doors. Flags hung limply in the still air above the entrance.

"Really?" Leo replied. "We're staying here? It's very nice!"

"Yep. I remember the hotel you booked for us in Hong Kong. I wasn't doing that again."

"There was nothing wrong with that," Leo replied, grabbing their bags and paying the taxi driver. "It had everything we needed and —"

Allissa had already stepped towards the hotel's revolving doors.

"There's something I need to sort out before I check in," Andreja said.

Leo and Allissa exchanged a glance.

"No problem," Allissa said. "The room's booked and pre-paid in your name. That shouldn't be an issue. You've got my number if you need anything."

"Thanks. Meet back here in two hours? We'll go get some food and discuss plans."

Leo and Allissa agreed.

Andreja turned, crossed the road and disappeared into the park opposite.

## 33

"What I'm offering is simple," Mikhail said, leaning back in his chair. He knitted his fingers together, and looked across the large oak desk at his guests on the other side. "You support my presidential campaign, and when I'm elected —"

"If you're elected," the man on the left interrupted.

Mikhail squinted at the man. "No! You see, Kozlova, you're not seeing the bigger picture here. You might own the biggest airline in this country, but what's the point of an airline if its planes are forbidden from flying?"

"You couldn't do that," the other man spat.

"Is that a gamble you're willing to take?"

The men stared at each other.

Mikhail continued, more softly. "Listen, we all want the same things, right? If you announce publicly that you're supporting me, when I win, I'll make sure you get any operating license you want, just like that." Mikhail snapped his fingers. "I'm going to win, anyway, and everyone wants to be on the winning team, do they not?"

The phone on the desk buzzed. Mikhail leaned forward

and pressed the button. His receptionist informed him he had an essential call.

"I must take this, gentlemen. Have a think about what we've discussed. You run a business this country is proud of. I would hate for you to run into problems."

The men rose from their seats and shuffled towards the door.

"Put the call through," Mikhail barked as the door thumped shut. The phone beeped and then buzzed.

"This is Mikhail. What do you want?"

"Mr Mikhail," came a nervous voice down the line. "I'm Erik Ronis. I'm an immigration officer at Riga International —"

"What do you want?" Mikhail demanded.

"A woman on the red list just entered the country. The system said that you were to be personally notified."

Mikhail shot forward, his elbows thumping to the desk.

"A woman called —" the man paused as though reading the name — "Panasenko, Andreja Panasenko."

"Interesting," Mikhail said, asking for the correct spelling of the name and writing it down. "Thank you Ronis, I'll check it out."

## 34

Leo and Allissa checked in. Then they showered, changed and were waiting outside the hotel two hours later. The gentle sound of music floated from somewhere nearby in the warm evening air. Buses and cars continued to stream past the hotel.

For Leo and Allissa it was something of a tradition to see a bit of the city on the first night. Getting a feel for the place was important in their work. It was also a welcome excuse to sit and drink a beer or three.

"Where is she?" Leo asked, glancing at the time on his phone. They'd been waiting twenty minutes already.

Allissa shrugged. "At least it's warm."

Leo glanced down at Allissa. She had a large hoodie draped around her shoulders, which Leo suspected may once have belonged to him.

"There, look!" Allissa said, pointing across the road. Andreja stood on the edge of the park, beckoning them across. She was almost invisible against the trees behind her.

"Good spot," Leo said.

They waited for two buses to rumble past and crossed the road.

"Sorry to keep you waiting," Andreja said. "I haven't been back for so long that I just couldn't wait to visit a couple of places. This way."

Before Leo or Allissa could reply, Andreja led them into the park. Thick darkness shrouded the trees and curvaceous streetlamps lit the paths in a dreamy glow.

Allissa glanced around. The beauty of the city was enchanting, and she was excited to be somewhere new.

"It's a beautiful place," Leo said as they reached a canal that curved through the parkland. "What does it feel like to be back?"

Andreja looked at Leo and smiled. "It's very strange. It has been such a long time. But it feels strangely like home too. I can't really explain it."

They walked side by side across an iron bridge. Allissa dropped a few coins into the guitar case of a man playing a tune she didn't recognise.

"Yeah, I can understand that," Leo said. "I bet the place has changed a bit."

"Yes, definitely. We didn't have visitors like this before." Andreja pointed at a group of young men staggering through the park. Leo presumed they were on holiday together.

"It has definitely got much more open. More westernised." Andreja directed them through a square with a franchise burger joint and a coffee house standing opposite each other.

"I suppose you can't have it both ways," Allissa mused. "You open up to the world, and you have to take the whole ugly lot of it."

The group of men noisily bundled their way through the

doors of a bar. Music thumped out until the door swung closed again.

"Exactly," Andreja said. "In 1993 people were crying out for it, though. Everyone here felt like they were missing some kind of party. Like the world was having all this fun, and we weren't invited. I bet in hindsight they wished they'd taken it all a bit more slowly."

Andreja led them down a thin cobbled road beside a vast church. A group of tourists in colourful clothes bustled the other way. Their laughter echoed from the antiquated architecture.

Allissa peered at couples dining by candlelight in a restaurant. Andreja turned down an even narrower passage. Allissa looked around and tried to remember from which direction they'd come.

"Here?" Andreja said, standing outside a bar with a vacant table on the pavement.

"Sure," Leo said. "I'll get the drinks. What would you like?"

Allissa and Andreja sat down. Leo arrived a few minutes later with a glass of wine for Andreja and pints of beer for Allissa and himself.

"You know, I wish I'd been able to find Emilija back then," Andreja said, looking at her hands. "I spent countless hours looking for her. In fact, I think that was the reason I wanted to come here at all. There was something in the back of my mind that niggled about where Emilija had gone."

Leo and Allissa took deep swigs of their pints. Leo nodded imperceptibly. Lacplesis was a good choice.

"The worst thing is, I don't even remember her clearly now. I was eight when we left Latvia, and she would've been six. Is that bad?" Her eyes locked on Allissa's.

"No, not at all," Allissa said, reaching out and touching Andreja's hand. "You were so young, no one would have remembered."

Andreja nodded morosely. "I should have hired someone, back in 1993. Someone like you guys who knew what they were doing."

"Why did you stop looking?" Leo asked.

"The exchange programme finished, and I had to return to England. I had a job lined up and everything was organised. Well, that was what I told myself, but you want to know the truth?" The green eyes swept across the table. Leo and Allissa nodded. "I'd given up. I'd convinced myself that she was dead, or so far away that I would never find her. I remember the week after I arrived, I said that to myself. If I don't make any progress in six months, I've just got to assume... you know? Is that awful? That really sounds —"

"No, that's totally understandable," Allissa said. "You needed to get on with your life. You couldn't have dedicated your whole life to it. That wouldn't have been fair at all."

Andreja nodded, picked up the glass and took two deep swallows. Leo and Allissa did the same. They were already halfway through their first pints. They were going down very well indeed.

"It sounds awful to say it now," Andreja said. "I know it does. But that's what I needed to do. I needed to have some kind of closure. The thing is, though, for you guys, in the UK, people going missing is rare. It's awful, but unusual. But growing up here under the Soviet Union, things were different. People did go missing and were often never seen again."

"Whatever happens," Allissa said, squeezing Andreja's hand. Andreja's eyes met Allissa's and then darted away. "Whatever happens, we will do all we can to get some answers for you. Those answers may not bring her back, but we will do everything in our power to find out what happened."

"I hope so," Andreja said, stone faced. "I can't face losing my home too."

Leo, Allissa and Andreja ate in fractured silence. Groups of revellers wandered past, their drunken voices raised in laughter or derision. Music pumped from a bar somewhere nearby.

Andreja finished eating and dug some money from her handbag. "I'm going to get straight back to the hotel," she said. "Today's wiped me out."

Allissa looked up at the woman, worry etched at the corner of her eyes.

"We'll come —"

"No, not at all. You guys stay here, have another drink, and relax. I'll be absolutely fine walking back on my own. It's much safer now than it was thirty years ago, believe me."

"Okay," Leo said. "We'll see you in the morning. I hope you get a good night's sleep."

Allissa agreed. "We'll get some answers for you soon."

"I hope so," Andreja said, looking down the passage, her expression steely. "I really hope so."

Then she turned and walked off into the darkened streets.

## 35

"What do you think, honestly?" Leo said, taking a sip from a fresh pint. "I mean, it's going to be a difficult one, isn't it?"

Allissa lifted the glass to her lips and nodded.

"Do you think she's still alive?"

Allissa inhaled and stared off into the distance. "I want to think so. I want to think we can find her living in a small village, cut off from the world, or something like that."

"No way," Leo said, taking another sip.

"No way what?"

"There's no way she's still alive after all this time. She's not been seen for over fifty years."

"That doesn't mean she's dead, though." Allissa took a sip of the beer. Her eyes met Leo's. "There're countless places she could be, and hundreds of things that could have happened. Why do you always think the worst?"

"I don't always think the worst. I'm just realistic. I don't mean to sound harsh, and of course I would never say this to the client, but there's no record of her in the last fifty years, so the chances are she's dead."

"Well, she might be dead. But there's an equal chance she's alive, working on a vineyard halfway up a mountain. Or herding goats. Or writing crosswords. Or any number of things."

"No way." Leo shook his head, his face lighting with a smile.

"Oh, I see, you're such an experienced investigator now that you just think about it for a few minutes and decide whether they're dead or alive." Allissa folded her arms. "No way. She's alive for sure."

"Well, I have been known to... you know..." Leo sipped his drink.

"What?"

"You know, just, uh, know stuff. You might call it magic, but for me it's just instinct."

Allissa laughed out loud. "Am I going to have to be careful, or else you'll put some voodoo hex on me?" Allissa shook in mock fear.

"Maybe. But no, seriously, don't you think you get that sort of feeling, that instinct?"

"I get a feeling when you're talking rubbish."

"Alright, ten quid." Leo stretched out his hand.

"Ten quid what?"

"Ten quid says that I'm right. Emilija is dead."

"You spineless bastard," Allissa hissed. Leo's expression dropped for a second.

"Make it fifty."

They shook hands, their fingers lingering together for a moment longer than normal. They exchanged smiles.

"You better start looking for remote mountainside goat farms," Leo said, taking a deep swig of the beer.

"You better start working out where you're going to get

my fifty quid from." Allissa downed the rest of her pint and stood up. "Come on then," she said.

Leo gulped down his drink.

Allissa rubbed her thumb and forefinger together. "I can feel that money now, but the look on your face is going to be worth even more."

## 36

Allissa revelled in the warming qualities of the alcohol as they stepped out onto the street. A group of men, obviously enjoying the effects of strong European beer too, staggered past.

"What time did we arrange to take the map to that guy?" Leo asked, walking alongside Allissa as they headed back in the general direction of their hotel.

"Tomorrow morning at eleven."

"He seemed pretty excited about it, didn't he?" Leo said. "I hope he can make sense of it. It's a long way to come if not."

"Getting nervous now, I see." Allissa smiled.

"Hell no," Leo replied. "What's Plan B?"

"We'll think of something." Allissa turned right down another smaller, medieval street. She glanced into a restaurant. Its chairs were stacked on the tables and two men mopped the floors. The dull thud of an electronic kick drum vibrated from a distant nightclub.

Allissa led them right again and through an archway

into a much smaller passageway. The shadows lay thick here, only broken by the occasional streetlight. Ahead, the passage turned sharply to the right.

Leo looked around. "You sure we're going the right way? I don't remember this from the way here."

Allissa paused and looked back the way they came. "No, you're right, nor do I. I think it was that way." She pointed further down the passage.

Allissa looped her arm through Leo's. They walked into the gloom. Reaching the corner, they followed the passage to the right. The cobbles underfoot were uneven. The passage ran straight ahead for as far as Allissa could see before dissolving into murkiness. The city, which just a few minutes ago was buoyed up by music and celebration, was now quiet and gloomy.

Allissa stopped and looked back the way they came again. That was as dark as the way forward. Leo stopped, too.

"I'm pretty sure —" Allissa stopped talking as footsteps resounded from the cobbles. Allissa was suddenly alert. Her eyes searched the shadows for any sign of movement. Nothing emerged. The footsteps died away.

"What is it?" Leo whispered, his voice urgent.

"Nothing, I just... I thought I heard something. Did you?" Allissa's voice was faint and brittle.

"I'm not sure... maybe... I —"

Ahead, a streetlight suddenly snapped on, bathing the passage in bright white light. Allissa's head whipped around, her eyes aching from the abrupt intrusion of light. She gasped and reeled backwards. They stumbled back into the shadows, their feet slipping on uneven cobbles.

In the island of light, just a few feet away, stood a man.

Despite the warm weather, he was dressed in a long, shapeless coat. The man stood motionless, his eyes on the floor in front of him. The streetlight cast unusual and eerie shadows across the face.

Leo and Allissa watched him, neither daring to speak.

Allissa's heart thundered beneath her ribs. She gripped Leo's hand.

Slowly, the man looked up at them. He was short and his eyes were widely spaced. He smiled, nodded, then clicked his fingers. A small dog scurried out from the shadows and stood at his heel. Then, nodding again, he bustled past Leo and Allissa and back into the labyrinthine passages. Somewhere beyond the buildings a tram clattered unseen. Loud music thumped.

Leo and Allissa emerged from the passage into a brightly lit square. The strong streetlights danced in front of their eyes for a few seconds. They stopped walking and exchanged glances. Neither wanted to admit what they'd suspected back in the passageway. This was a fifty-year-old case. No one was watching them. No one even cared they were here.

Allissa cleared her throat and shook her head, as though trying to clear the unhelpful thoughts away.

"It was so dark back there," she said, trying and failing to sound cheerful. Fear etched its way into her voice.

"Yeah, it was a bit, sort of, eerie, wasn't it?"

Leo and Allissa locked eyes, both sure that the other had the same concerns. Neither wanted to say them out loud.

"Yeah, it is a bit." Allissa nodded. "Let's get back to the hotel. It's this way I think."

Both took several deep breaths as they crossed the square.

Behind them, a couple jostled out through the door of a

franchise coffee bar. Their voices, speaking in a language Leo and Allissa didn't understand, reverberated against the surrounding buildings. The couple laughed about something, paused to decide on which direction to go, and disappeared into a backstreet.

After a few steps, Allissa started to feel better. She glanced back at the alleyway from which they'd emerged. It was nothing, surely. A man out walking his dog. There was nothing suspicious about that.

Leo and Allissa, now relaxing into the pace of the city, walked past a giant column. A copper statue of a woman on the zenith held three golden stars towards the sky. Leo and Allissa paused to glance up at the structure before heading back through the park towards their hotel.

Leo unlocked the door and snapped on the light. Their bags lay beside three coiled towels on the bed. Leo padded across the thick carpet and looked out at the city through the window. The tip of the monument — the three shining stars — loomed a few hundred yards away above the dark shapes of the trees. Thick curtains framed the windows.

"It's a nice room," Leo said, all anxiety fading as the lock clicked shut. "Please don't tell me how much it cost."

"I won't," Allissa said, walking towards Leo, putting her arms around his waist, and hugging him. Now she was inside she felt fine, too. Maybe just tired, that was all.

Leo smiled. "Thanks. What's that for?"

"You know, just because I... I wanted to. I can hug my... you, if I want to, right?"

"Of course you can. Anytime you like." Leo turned, put his arms around Allissa, pulled her tight and looked out at the city. Dark parkland sprawled out before them, beyond which the ornate rooftops of the city crowded for attention.

"Let's go to bed," Allissa said, breaking off the hug and stepping towards the giant bed.

Leo's eyes followed her hungrily, and something lurched in his stomach. His breathing became tight for all the right reasons.

## 37

Allissa's heart pumped iron as she ran. Her legs stung with each thump of the uneven ground.

She gasped for air. Each breath was ragged and futile in the humid night.

She reached a corner and charged around it. This alley was just as narrow as the last one. Boxes, rubbish and other detritus was piled up on both sides.

Allissa glanced behind her with a panicked flick of the head. She longed to see her pursuers. Nothing was visible in the darkness. Vague shapes moved together. But there were voices, raised voices, coming her way.

Allissa smashed through a pile of trash. Something sharp ripped against her shin. Glass crunched beneath her feet. A white-hot pain jarred through her body. She gritted her teeth and ran harder. Faster.

She couldn't get distracted now. She had to concentrate at putting her feet on solid ground. She straightened up and pumped her legs.

The following voices were closer now. They shouted

unknown words. She wasn't going to risk losing her footing by looking again.

She reached a crossroads. An eerie orange light glowed from somewhere. Without thinking, Allissa charged left.

Her legs burned like hot knives. She tasted acid in her mouth. She ran some more.

This street was like the last, but darker. Just another dusty street with the occasional island of light. Faceless street after faceless street.


ALLISSA WOKE in the giant hotel bed, panting and covered in a film of sweat. She gasped several times in the silent room and pushed up onto her elbows. The covers were twisted around her. She kicked her legs free of the blanket.

Allissa snapped on the bedside lamp, and bright white light bathed the room.

She glanced at Leo beside her, snoring softly. She was glad that her thrashing about hadn't woken him up.

She looked at the clock on the bedside table. It was just after three am.

It was unusual for Allissa to be woken by nightmares. In fact, her problem had always been the opposite. Even multiple alarms couldn't permeate the deep stupor in which she slept. That was until about six months ago and their case in New York.

Allissa instinctively ran her fingers across her neck, where the killer's knife had been ready to do its work. A knife held by a madman. A crazed lunatic who would have killed her without Leo's intervention.

She glanced again at Leo sleeping beside her, and smiled.

The dreams would pass, she was sure of that. They were

safe here, and she was doing what she loved. She wouldn't let some madman, who would now spend the rest of his life in prison, change how she led her life.

Smiling, Allissa settled back into the bed and closed her eyes.

Two gruff male voices seeped through the door. Uneven footsteps shuffled down the corridor. A door slammed.

Allissa didn't notice as she drifted back off into a dreamless sleep.

## 38

"Morning," Leo said, placing a steaming cup of coffee on the bedside table beside Allissa. "We need to get going soon. We're meeting Andreja in the foyer at ten, remember?"

"What time is it?" Allissa moaned. Her eyes opened slowly. Leo had opened the curtains and bright morning light lay in a thick beam across the bed. The roofs and treetops of the city glimmered through the window.

"A little after nine. I'm going to jump in the shower. You drink that and wake up."

Leo smiled at Allissa's grumpy morning face, then turned and padded into the bathroom. Allissa forced herself to sit up, snatched up the coffee and took a big sip.

Forty-five minutes later, by the miraculous properties of caffeine and Leo's expert nagging, they were waiting in the hotel foyer. Allissa lounged back into one of the leather sofas, while Leo examined the large oil paintings that adorned the walls.

A man in a grey uniform ran a hoover across the thick crimson carpet. The revolving door spun, admitting a small gulp of outside traffic noise with each quarter revolution. A couple dressed in fine clothes swanned from the door and flounced across to the reception desk.

The second hand of the large brass clock on the far wall made its final climb to the top of the hour. Allissa watched it closely, considering all the seconds she could have been asleep, rather than here.

"She'll be here any minute," Leo said, turning from the painting of a horse pulling a canon up a hill. "I don't think she'll be late. She was more excited about this than we were."

Allissa nodded, leaned forward and snatched up a newspaper from the coffee table. She flicked through the pages. It was in Latvian and unsurprisingly made no sense to her. Many of the pictures contained serious-looking old men making speeches.

The cleaner finished his work and turned off the hoover. He pushed through a door marked *staff only,* dragging the hoover behind him. Traffic hummed quietly past the main doors.

"I'll call her, maybe she's forgotten." Leo tugged his phone from his pocket.

Allissa looked up at the large clock. It was approaching half past. "She's probably just slept in," Allissa said, folding the paper and throwing it back on the table. Somewhere within her, the first buds of disquiet poked above the surface. This wasn't something she had expected.

Leo found the number and held the phone to his ear. The phone rang ten times and then, as though tormenting him, cut to silence.

"Okay, now that's strange," Leo said.

"I'll go back to the room and check on her." Allissa climbed to her feet. "You wait here in case she comes back."

"Sure, yeah. Good idea," Leo agreed.

Allissa headed in the direction of the stairs. She reached the fourth floor quickly. Andreja's room was just down the corridor from theirs. Brass plaques with the room numbers shone from each of the doors. Allissa stood to the side as a maid came the other way, sliding a trolley stacked high with clean bedding.

Allissa reached Andreja's door and knocked. The sound echoed dully through the room inside. Allissa stepped back from the door and waited. Seconds passed. There was no response. Allissa's budding sense of disquiet grew further. She looked left and right. The maid had stopped four doors down to turn over the room for its next occupants.

Allissa stepped up to the door and thumped against the wood again. "Andreja, you in there?" Allissa shouted. There was no reply. Allissa slid out her phone — no contact from Leo or Andreja.

She thumped against door one more time, as loud as she could this time. No one could sleep through that. Long, silent moments passed. There was no reply.

Allissa swore under her breath and remembered the unsettling sense of the previous night. Now there was no sign of Andreja.

A maid returned to the trolley with a bundle of sheets for the laundry.

"Excuse me," Allissa shouted, running up to her. "I'm locked out of my room. Could you let me in please?"

The young lady looked at Allissa blankly.

Allissa pointed towards the door and mimed the losing of her key.

The young lady's expression hardened for a moment. She looked sternly at Allissa.

"I'm so sorry." Allissa smiled as sweetly as the worry would allow.

"*Ja, ja,*" the young woman said, nodding as she pulled a key card from her apron and swiped it in the lock.

"Thank you, thank you," Allissa said. A green light on the locking mechanism flashed.

The maid slouched off down the corridor and Allissa pushed open the door.

"Hello, Andreja, it's Allissa. Are you okay?"

Allissa stepped inside the room. The door closed behind her.

With the thick curtains drawn, the room was gloomy.

Allissa snapped on the light. Her eyes sprang wide. Her hands shot to her mouth. Her drop of worry flowed into a full ocean of panic.

## 39

Leo examined each of the foyer's paintings then set about looking through a stack of leaflets on a side table. Someone rattled through the revolving door. Leo's head whipped around, expecting to see Allissa or Andreja. A man in a grey suit strode towards the reception desk.

Leo glanced up at the clock. It was now gone half ten.

His phone vibrated. Leo dropped the leaflet, advertising a modern art exhibition, and dug out his phone. It took him several seconds to extract it from his pocket and hold it to his ear.

"Leo." Allissa's voice was a harsh whisper. "You need to get up here now."

"Are you okay?"

"Yes, yes, I'm fine. But you need to get here."

Leo charged across to the lifts and thumbed the call buttons. Both lifts were on the upper floors and showed no signs of movement. Leo gave up after a few seconds and ran for the stairs. Banging through the door on the fourth floor, he darted towards Andreja's room. The door was ajar. He pushed it open and stepped inside.

"There was no answer, and I got the maid to open it for me," Allissa said, standing in the middle of the room. She stood rigid, as though expecting something awful to happen. Leo stepped further into the room.

Leo gasped.

The room had been ransacked. The mattress lay against one wall, the sheets and pillows torn from it. The cupboard doors and drawers were open. Andreja's bag lay discarded on its side. Her clothes littered the floor. A lamp was twisted and shattered, its glass on the carpet below. Two chairs lay on their sides. Broken glass, sachets of coffee, tea, and products from the bathroom were scattered across the floor.

Leo looked from the devastation to Allissa. He swallowed. His throat was suddenly dry.

"They've taken Andreja," Allissa said, her voice soft and weak.

"And they've taken the map," Leo added. Allissa turned. They locked eyes.

"No," Allissa replied, "they tried to take the map, but with the room like this, my betting is they couldn't find it."

## 40

"If you were Andreja," Leo said as he walked around the room, "where would you hide something in here?"

"I wouldn't," Allissa said, surveying the devastation.

"I know, but I mean, what if you had to?"

"I still wouldn't hide it in here. There are only so many places something can be hidden in a hotel room, and they're all pretty easy to search. If I wanted to hide something, I'd put it somewhere else for sure."

Leo sunk into a crouch and looked up at the surrounding room. "Yes, you're right, but that assumes one thing —"

"Andreja expected people to be looking for this map."

Leo nodded. Two people walked down the corridor; their voices streamed through the thin door. They passed, and the sound drifted back into the murmur of the air conditioning and the hum of traffic outside.

"Let's get out of here," Allissa said. She suddenly felt very exposed in the room. Her eyes darted towards the door.

"There's nothing here and whoever did this might come back."

Allissa crossed the room and peered out through the door. The bright corridor was empty. She and Leo stepped out and pulled the door closed behind them. They forced themselves to walk slowly the short distance back to their room. Leo paused outside their door. He looked one way and then the other. When he was sure no one was looking, he dug out his key card and unlocked the door.

As the lock clicked shut, Allissa pulled a deep breath.

"We need to think," Leo said, pacing to the window and back again. "The people who took Andreja wanted the information she had, right?"

"How would they know she had that information?"

Leo stopped walking and turned to face Allissa. "If the location of these files is so important, it could be what guaranteed Marija safe passage out of the country back in the seventies. That could have been her bargaining chip, so to speak."

Allissa agreed. "Maybe what Jansons said is right, someone in power right now really doesn't want these files to come out, so they've put some kind of alert on anyone associated with them entering the country."

"That's got to be a seriously powerful person." Leo stopped walking and glanced around the room. "Hold on, what if they're listening to us now?" His fists clenched.

"Why would they?" Allissa asked.

"Because we're here with Andreja, obviously."

"Wait a second, think about it," Allissa said. "At passport control, Andreja made sure she was in a separate queue. We got the same taxi together, but that could just be a coincidence. She even met us on the other side of the road. All the while we were walking, she was twenty feet ahead —"

"Yeah, that did seem strange at the time."

"Andreja chose the table in the restaurant. I bet she was thinking of security cameras or something."

"And we checked in separately," Leo added. "Remember, Andreja said she had something to do?"

"Wait a minute, what did you say?" Allissa spun to face at Leo. "Just then, what did you say?"

"Andreja said she had something to do, remember? She didn't come into the hotel with us, she walked off in the other direction, and then —"

Leo was interrupted by a sound. His breath caught in his throat and his stomach turned to lead. There was a knock at the door.

## 41

"Who's that?" Leo whispered, glancing from the door to Allissa.

Allissa shrugged.

The knock came again, reverberating aggressively into the room.

"We're going to have to answer it," Allissa said. "Coming," she shouted.

"No wait." Leo pictured the destruction a few doors away. He scanned the room for something he could use as a weapon should they need it. He grabbed an ornate china lamp from the bedside table and stood behind the door.

For once, Allissa didn't roll her eyes.

"Okay," Leo said, raising the lamp above his head. "Open the door, slowly."

Allissa turned the handle. The mechanism clicked. The door squeaked softly. A young woman in a uniform of the hotel smiled at Allissa.

"Miss Stockwell, I have your dry cleaning," she said, holding up a trouser suit Allissa had never seen before.

Allissa stuttered over her answer, then glanced at Leo,

who nodded. "Yes, thank you, that almost slipped my mind," Allissa said.

"You're welcome, miss." The young woman handed Allissa the suit. "Oh, one more thing, these were in the pockets. Lucky someone checked. They wouldn't have been much good to you after they'd been through the washer." She handed over a few receipts stapled together. "Could you just sign here, please?"

Allissa signed with the offered pen and the woman bustled off back towards the lifts. Allissa stepped back into the room and shut the door. She looked at Leo and shook her head slowly. A smile bloomed across her face.

"What was that about?" Leo asked, replacing the lamp and rushing back to Allissa. "You didn't do any —"

"Look," Allissa said, holding up the stapled papers. "This one's a receipt for left luggage," she said.

## 42

Jansons leaned back, and the chair creaked beneath him. The midmorning light piled in through the window in thick squares. All the windows were open, and the flat was still oppressively hot. He undid another button on his shirt and pulled the material away from his clammy skin.

The lock he'd been servicing lay in various pieces on the table-top. It was a simple job, but today Jansons couldn't seem to concentrate.

He glanced at the clock on the wall by the kitchen. The second hand shuddered in the direction of midday. The British detectives were supposed to have been here nearly an hour ago.

Jansons climbed to his feet and padded through to the apartment's front door. He peered through the viewing hole at the corridor outside. It was empty, as he knew it would be. He had an early warning system that detected motion at the end of the corridor.

He strode back into the living room and gazed out through the blinds. A hatchback car, one of those Japanese things, slid quietly past his apartment. A woman with a pushchair walked in the sun. Everything was quiet. Nothing raised his suspicions.

Maybe they had just got delayed. That was not uncommon. Jansons slumped back into his seat, pulled a cigarette from the packet, and lit it. The end flared, and he dragged a deep lungful of smoke.

People got delayed all the time, for all sorts of reasons. It was nothing to worry about, he told himself.

## 43

"But if she thought this might happen, why didn't she tell us? Why did she even want to come in the first place?" Leo said, as they crossed the canal, following the directions on Allissa's phone towards the Riga Left Luggage office.

"She wasn't happy that we were coming, was she?" Allissa said. "I think maybe she was trying to protect us. If we started poking around and asking questions, we could have got into trouble."

A man walked past with a takeaway coffee, a dog pulling on its lead. A young woman swished past on an electric scooter. The boisterous night-time city was quiet and sedate by daylight. It was both refined and interesting, and Leo liked it. For a moment he wished, as he often did, that they could just enjoy these places.

Riga Left Luggage lay down a backstreet in the shadow of one of the city's many vast churches. Leo glanced up at the spire, rugged against the deep blue sky. He looked right and left. The street was empty. A sense of unease broiled in his stomach.

The shop was in the basement, below a hostel.

Allissa descended the stairs and pushed open the door. A bell jangled. Leo stepped in after her. It was oppressively hot inside. Leo's chest tightened with the enclosed space and thin air.

A counter split the room in half. Behind the counter, shelves were stacked high with bags and suitcases of various colours. Posters of Riga's multiple attractions covered the walls.

"Hello, one moment," came a friendly, accented male voice. A flurry of typing keys followed. "Done. Sorry about that." A small man with dark hair and tiny round glasses appeared from a door at the side. "Are you here to deposit or collect?"

"Collect please." Allissa slid the receipt across the counter.

The man picked it up and examined it. He glanced up at Allissa and then looked down at the receipt again. "Ahh, yes, I see. 224. Let's see here." The man turned and paced down the line of shelves. "220, 222," he muttered, tapping his chin. "Here we are. 224."

Leo's chest tightened. For the first time since they'd arrived, the idea of just turning around, going back to the airport, and going home occurred to him. Leo rejected it. They weren't going to do that. He clenched his fists and counted out his breathing slowly. He was better than this now. They were better than this. They would find Andreja and learn what had happened to her sister. Leo pulled another deep breath and counted it in for four seconds.

The man removed a shopping bag from the shelf. He placed his hands beneath the bag as though it were heavy and sidled back towards the counter. Allissa peered eagerly at it. The bag contained a box that was about twelve inches square.

The man asked Allissa to sign something and placed the bag on the counter. Allissa glanced inside. *Vina Kalns* was printed on a brown cardboard box. The box chinked as Allissa moved it. She eagerly pulled open the lid. There were six bottles of wine inside. She tilted the box to show Leo, and they exchanged confused glances.

"Very good choice," the man said, his eyes darting down towards the box.

"Sorry?" Allissa said.

"This wine. Made in Latvia. Very nice."

"Yes." Allissa forced a smile. "A friend of ours said that we must try it. Thank you."

Allissa picked up the box, the bottles rattling, and clambered up the stairs behind Leo to the street.

"She sent us to collect six bottles of wine?" Leo said, looking at the box Allissa carried against her stomach. "What are we supposed to do with that?"

"Hold on," Allissa said, crossing to a bench. "There may be more than just wine in here. Andreja may have thought it suspicious just to leave a folder of documents in the left luggage place."

Allissa placed the box of wine on the bench and sat down beside it.

Leo glanced around the street again, and, satisfied that no one nearby was watching, sat beside Allissa.

Allissa pulled back the plastic bag and flipped open the lid of the box. She pulled out the bottles one at a time and checked the box carefully. Nothing. The box contained only the six bottles of wine.

"What the hell," Leo said, peering closely inside the box. "There's nothing there."

"Hold on a minute," Allissa said, pulling out one of the bottles. The golden writing on the label shone in the light. "It's a clue. This is the wine Andreja had in her house. This is the wine we used to soak the pages of the notebook."

Leo pulled out another bottle. "Yes, I think you're right. But what does that mean?"

"It means we know where to go next." Allissa drew a receipt from the bag. "Ozolin's Wine Merchants," she read out loud.

## 44

A quick online search showed that Ozolin's Wine Merchants was only three streets away.

"How long did she have to put this together?" Allissa said, leading them with the map on her phone. Leo lumbered beside her, carrying the box.

"Two hours, including walking to and from the hotel. She must have planned it before."

Allissa agreed. Andreja was becoming a more complex character by the moment. Allissa turned through an archway and down a narrow-cobbled street. The sky was reduced to a thin strip of blue between the overhanging buildings on both sides.

"We're here." Allissa stopped abruptly. Her eyes darted from her phone to the surrounding buildings. Darkened windows gazed down from above them. Sheer walls of ancient brick towered skywards.

Leo looked around too. His arms ached from the weight of the wine.

"There, look."

A sign hung above a tiny door on the right of the

passage. The door was no higher than Leo's chin. Both had assumed it was nothing more than a back entrance to some house or shop on a neighbouring street.

*Ozolin's Wine Merchants.* The washed out words were barely readable.

Leo glanced at Allissa. Excitement shone in her eyes.

Allissa approached the door and knocked. The sound was muted by the thick wooden door, blackened by many years of decay. Allissa tapped again. No reply.

"Try the door," Leo said, his arms burning now. "See if it's open."

Allissa did. The heavy mechanism clunked, and the door swung open. Allissa flashed a smile at Leo. Leo couldn't help but smile back, although his arms ached and now his nerves flared. The last time they'd walked through a door like this, awful things happened.

Allissa pushed the door open further. A narrow passage led down a set of vertiginous steps. The walls, floor and ceiling were constructed with the same golden bricks as the front of the building. A series of bare, low wattage bulbs glowed orange from fixtures on the walls.

"These things just keep happening to us, don't they?" Allissa said, as though reading Leo's mind. Then, without hesitation, she stepped inside.

"Yes," Leo said, his arms now throbbing from the dead weight of the wine. "You'd think we'd learn not to keep getting involved."

## 45

Allissa took the stairs slowly, using the wall for support.

Leo glanced along the passage, one way and then the other. They were alone. The box of wine slid from his sweaty grasp. He gripped it tighter, took a deep breath and followed Allissa through the door and down the steep staircase. Their footsteps reverberated from the bare walls.

The door slammed shut behind them. Leo, startled by the sound, glanced towards it, and almost lost his footing on the precipitous staircase. The hum of the city faded.

"What is this place?" Allissa whispered, reaching the bottom of the stairs. She turned and noticed Leo struggling down the stairs behind her. His face was reddened by exertion and his growing anxiety. "Are you okay? Can I help you with that?"

"No, no, it's fine," Leo said, panting, working hard to control his breathing. He reached the bottom of the staircase. The air tasted different here. It was cool and carried with it an unfamiliar rich aroma.

Ahead of them stood a door with several glass panels,

each showing a distorted snatch of the room inside. Allissa pushed open the door and strode inside. A bell jangled somewhere. The smell of dried flowers hung in the air.

The room Allissa stepped into was long and thin. It was perhaps twenty feet wide, but two or three times that in length. The vaulted ceiling, walls, and bare floors were constructed from the same golden stone as the stairs they'd just descended. Throughout the room, dark wooden shelves displayed bottles of wine, each carefully illuminated with beams of orange light.

"Hello," Allissa said, looking around. No reply came. She wandered up to one of the displays of bottles. Golden labels shone beneath the spotlights. She examined one that looked grander than the others.

"That's a 1993 vintage from Vīna Kalns. A special bottle to commemorate our independence. I've had a few people offer to buy it, but I've never been able to let it go." A mellifluous voice carried through the rose-scented air. Allissa spun on her heels.

A man stood at the end of the room. Everything about his appearance was grey. His suit, hair and beard all took on the hue of storm clouds or battle ships. Even the pallor of his skin was tinged the colour of fresh concrete.

Allissa tried to consider his age but drew a blank between about forty and sixty-five.

"But I don't expect you'll want to buy that. I've had it valued in the region of ten to fifteen thousand euro. To be honest with you, I'm not even sure it would taste that good anymore." The man took two steps forward. "Matiss Ozolin. Welcome to my humble store. How can I help you?" The grey man leaned towards Allissa.

"Fifteen thousand euro? That's a lot… " Allissa glanced at the bottle again. "No, we'd like to ask you something."

Leo slid the box of wine on to a table. He wiped the sweat from his hands and attempted to shake the feeling back into his fingers.

"We're trying to trace the lady who bought this box of wine from you yesterday." Allissa pointed at the box. "It's really important we find her as soon as possible."

Ozolin swanned across the room and examined the box. "Yesterday, you say?" He smiled up at Leo.

"Yes, sometime in the early evening," Leo replied.

Ozolin's mouth pursed in thought. Suddenly his eyes lit with a realisation. His long index finger unfurled from his hand and pointed at a shelf on the far side of the room. "That's where this wine is stored. I'll check the register. I should have a record of when this sale was made."

"Thank you," Allissa said. Slightly confused by the man's directions, she turned and crossed to the far corner.

Ozolin strode silently to the other side of the room and disappeared behind a thick velvet curtain.

"Grab one of those bottles," Allissa said.

Leo slid one of the bottles from the box and carried it across the room.

The bottles were packed more tightly here. Various varieties and vintages filled the shelves. Leo and Allissa searched the top shelf for the matching label. Nothing. They switched their attention to the one below. Again, none of the bottles matched those in the box. They scanned the third shelf and again came up with nothing. Leo sunk to a crouch and examined the bottles on the bottom shelf.

"There it is!" Allissa was first to notice the bottles. Several of them squatted on the far side of the shelf, almost shrouded in shadow. Allissa glanced excitedly at Leo. She was unable to verbalise what she saw. She pointed frantically at the bottles. Leo crouched down further and saw what she was looking at.

Careful not to knock any of the bottles, he reached in and extracted the folder containing what they both knew to be Marija's secret map.

## 46

Leo looked down at the folder in his hands, not quite registering why Andreja had left it on a shelf in an underground wine store.

"Yes, so," Ozolin's smooth voice carried through the room again, "that box of wine was sold at six fifteen yesterday evening." He crossed the room and pointed at the box. "It's a great choice too. One of my favourite table wines."

Leo and Allissa looked up towards the voice. Leo glanced down at the folder in his hands. Allissa stepped to the right, obscuring Leo from the wine merchant. Leo shrugged off his rucksack and slipped the folder inside.

"Thank you," Leo said. "That's been really helpful. Now we've at least got a time we know she was here."

"Yes, we've got something to work from now. That's really helpful." Allissa strode towards the door.

Leo swung his bag over his shoulder and crossed to the door.

"It's my pleasure," Ozolin said reverently.

Allissa grabbed the door handle and pulled the door

open. The bell jangled. She stepped through and climbed the stairs towards the street.

"Thanks," Leo said again, following Allissa towards the staircase.

"Wait a minute," Ozolin's voice boomed up the staircase. Leo and Allissa froze.

Leo's breath caught in his throat. The muscles of his legs tightened in preparation to run or fight. The straps of the bag containing the folder seemed to tighten around his shoulders.

"You've left your wine," Ozolin said.

"Oh, yes." Leo exhaled. "Are we able to leave it here and collect it when we've finished our business?"

"I... well... that is very unusual, but I suppose I can keep it in the office for you, yes."

Ozolin smiled as the two English detectives climbed the stairs and out towards the street. The noise of the city streamed down the passageway and dimmed again as the door swung shut. He picked up the box of wine and carried it back behind the velvet curtain.

"Very good," he said to the silent room in his native Latvian. "Much quicker than expected, too."

## 47

Leo and Allissa took the stairs two at a time and emerged from the small black door and out into the still deserted passageway. Leo pulled several greedy breaths of the warm afternoon air.

They both looked around carefully. Somewhere in another street a tram clanged around a corner.

"I think we need to make a plan," Leo said.

Allissa agreed.

They turned right, then left and emerged on to a wide pavement. Traffic roared down a dual carriageway and the grey surface of the Daugava River glittered in the sun beyond. Allissa led them across the road and stood at the railing, looking out at the river. She glanced around.

A woman in pink sportswear ran past. Three young people whizzed past on bikes. There was nothing to suggest they were being watched now, although Allissa couldn't shake the sensation that someone was nearby. She put it to the back of her mind and gazed out at the river's quicksilver surface. To their left, a blue and yellow train rumbled through the iron arches of the railway bridge.

"We have to assume then that Andreja knew people would come for her," Leo said. His hands tightened around the rucksack's straps. He turned and scanned the surrounding area for anyone looking their way. He glanced at a bin a few yards away. He resisted the urge to stuff the folder in it and forget about the whole thing.

"Yes, I think it's fair to say that the people who took Andreja want these documents. They wouldn't have torn her room apart looking for them if not, and she wouldn't have gone to all those lengths to hide them."

Leo nodded. A large boat slid regally beneath the railway bridge.

"The question is, what do we do about them?" Leo said. "We can't even arrange a trade because we don't know who they are."

"But that wouldn't get us any closer to finding out what happened to Emilija. That's why we're here, remember."

Leo nodded. "There's only one thing to do. We have to find out where this map leads. Then we'll find the truth about Emilija and find out where Andreja is too."

Allissa looked up at Leo. "That's exactly what we need to do," she said, reaching up on her tiptoes and kissing him on the cheek.

"Where do we start?" Leo asked.

"Let's go and see the locksmith."

## 48

The train juddered and wheezed into Zolitūde Station. The doors whooshed open. The passengers waiting on the platform lurched forwards, as though the train was going to speed away without warning.

Leo and Allissa fought their way down onto the platform and looked around. Beyond the graffiti-marked station building, several concrete apartment blocks stood dark and solid against the sky. Each of the blocks was ten stories high. From this distance, it was impossible to tell where one apartment complex began and the other ended. Scarred with satellite dishes, broken windows and rusting window bars, they were a world away from the grand architecture of the city centre.

Leo and Allissa stepped into the shadows of the single-storey station building. Allissa dug out her phone and programmed Jansons' address into the sat nav. Leo watched the final few people climb down from the train. He searched for any casual glance in their direction that might give their follower away. He saw nothing. The people on their tail were each too clever for that, or they were not being followed at all. Leo hoped it was the latter.

"This way," Allissa said as the map loaded and pointed them in the right direction. She led them around the station building and across a crumbling expanse of tarmac, presumably used as a car park.

They crossed a road and walked into the shadow of one of the apartment blocks. Leo gazed up at the countless dark windows.

For fifteen minutes they weaved between different apartment complexes, each of which looked identical, as though they'd been fired in the same mould. Unsure why, Leo found it strangely unsettling.

"Here." Allissa stopped and pointed up at one of the buildings. "Apartment 105, first floor."

Leo pulled open the door, and they walked into a dark concrete stairwell. They hustled up to the first floor, their footsteps echoing from the concrete walls.

A door slammed somewhere above. The sound thundered around the enclosed space. A male voice shouted something, and a female answered. Footsteps pummelled down the stairs.

Leo's eyes adjusted to the gloom now. He saw the door to apartment 102 on their left.

"This way," he said, leading Allissa down a corridor away from the staircase.

The descending footsteps reverberated closer.

Light seeped in from a dirty window at the end of the corridor.

Leo stopped outside apartment 105.

The footsteps continued.

Leo rapped his knuckles against the door of apartment

105. The thin door rattled against its fixings. The sound blared in the empty corridor. Leo glanced at Allissa.

Apartment 105 remained silent.

The descending footsteps passed the first floor, and then the door on the ground floor opened. The footsteps thumped outside, and the door creaked closed again.

Leo stepped forward to pound on the door again. Footsteps shuffled nearby. A lock clunked. Leo examined the door closely. Nothing moved. Another lock snapped, and then another. The door to apartment 105 still didn't move.

"You were supposed to be here at ten." A voice boomed out into the hallway.

Leo and Allissa whipped around to face the voice. A grey-haired man peered at them from the door of apartment 107.

Leo pointed to apartment 105, which was now behind them.

"We're here to see Jansons? Is he —?"

"Get in here," the man snarled, swinging open the door and standing aside. "Before anyone sees you, quickly."

Leo and Allissa glanced at each other and then followed the man's instructions. He showed them into what Leo assumed was the apartment's largest room. A window overlooked a strip of grass opposite. Beside the window, a door led onto a small balcony. A gentle breeze drifted through the open door.

"I wouldn't be stupid enough to give you the actual address of my apartment," Jansons said, lowering himself onto a wooden dining chair. Several locks were spread out on the Formica table before him. Leo noticed how ordered the items on the table-top were. A dozen different screwdrivers and other tools were lined up to the right. A small pot of oil and a cloth sat at the top, and to the left, a lit cigarette smouldered in the ashtray.

Jansons snagged up the cigarette and pulled a lungful.

"Sit down, sit down." He waved a hand at a brown sofa, which sagged dangerously close to the floor. "You don't know who might be listening on those things." Jansons pointed at his phone on the table by the window. "There are ears everywhere, you know? Everywhere."

Allissa lowered herself carefully into the sofa. The old springs protested with a squeal. "We need your help with something, Mr Jansons. I'm afraid things have got rather more complicated since we spoke on the phone."

Leo slipped off his rucksack, placed it on the floor, and sat down beside Allissa.

Jansons' eyebrows arched as Allissa explained about Andreja's disappearance and the destruction in her hotel room.

"I knew it," he said, his clenched fist banging an erratic pattern on his knee. "I knew it. It's these files, I've told you. These missing files. They must think that Marija kept a record — "

"How would Marija have a record of these files? I thought she worked at the university?" Leo asked.

Jansons roared with laughter. A laugh that quickly turned into a hacking cough.

"Yes, she did," he said when the cough had subsided. "But it wasn't a university like you would expect. Many of the government's secret operations were housed there. Sort of" — Jansons drew circles with his cigarette while he searched for the words — "a front. A cover. Marija was clever enough, or stupid enough, to keep a record of the information she was passing across. She used that to make a deal for her extradition. Very smart move I think." He went to take a drag on the cigarette, but it had gone out. With surprising speed, Jansons fished a lighter from his pocket and relit it.

"But why would someone go to the effort of abducting Andreja for this now?" Allissa asked. "This was back in the seventies, right? And Andreja came to Riga in the nineties with no problems."

"Ah," Jansons said, holding up his yellowed finger. "Because it is a very sensitive time now. Next month is the election for a new president." Jansons picked up a newspaper, unfolded it, and pointed at the picture on the front page. A grey-haired man, probably in his seventies, stood with his arms outstretched in speech. "Johanson Mikhail. He is the favourite to win. In the seventies he was a colonel in the Committee for State Security of the Latvian Soviet Socialist Republic. Absolutely ruthless."

"The KGB?" Leo probed.

"If you want to call it that. There are rumours that he caused the death or disappearance of nearly a thousand people, including Emilija Panasenko and her father, Peteris Panasenko."

"If Mikhail found out Andreja was back in the country, and thought there was some outside chance that she had these records, he would do everything he could to stop her, right?" Leo said.

"Correct. He is a very powerful man. Lots of money. Lots of influence. He could very easily —"

An electronic buzz came from the direction of the door. Jansons was suddenly alert. His eyes darted towards the door. He leapt to his feet with a speed that belied his age.

"What's that?" Allissa asked, seeing his agitation.

"A motion detector outside the door. Someone is coming."

"One of your neighbours, maybe?" Leo suggested.

"No," Jansons snarled, glancing at Leo with fire in his eyes. "The other apartments in this corridor are empty. Someone has followed you here."

## 49

Beyond the electronic buzz, feet shuffled in the corridor.

Jansons rushed about the apartment. His wild eyes glanced at the door every second or two. He stuffed various things into his jacket pockets.

"Come on," he hissed in a loud whisper. "We've got to get out of here."

Leo and Allissa struggled from the sofa. Leo grabbed his rucksack and slipped it on.

A knock followed. A heavy fist against thin wood. Leo's heart skipped a beat. He looked from Jansons to the door, then to the window, and finally at Allissa.

"They'll search the other apartment first," Jansons snarled. "But it won't take them long to come this way."

The sound of splintering wood reverberated through the door. Feet shuffled forwards. Leo imagined the men who had taken Andreja storming inside the opposite apartment. The familiar grasp of anxiety tightened his chest. A strand of barbed wire surrounded his heart. His muscles tightened and his legs begged him to run.

"How... how..." Leo stuttered. In his mind's eye, the men had already crashed through the door and were dragging them away to some windowless cell.

"Don't worry," Jansons said, a wry smile lighting his face. "I've prepared for this." Jansons rushed over to the door and silenced the buzzer. He disappeared inside the bedroom and emerged a moment later with a small bag slung over his shoulder.

"This way," he said, striding through the door onto the tiny balcony.

The stoop with which Jansons had previously moved had all but disappeared. The man now moved with confidence and strength.

More feet shuffled in the corridor outside the door. A whispered voice rose above the noise. A strong hand thundered against the door.

The coil of barbed wire dug further into Leo's chest. He exchanged a panicked glance with Allissa. They followed Jansons out on to the small balcony. Even though they were only on the first floor, the drop to the road below was at least twenty feet.

Jansons glanced behind him, his lips parted in a smile, and then hopped over the wall and disappeared.

Leo and Allissa rushed forward and peered over the wall. Six feet below, Jansons stood on a flat roof that extended out from the side of the building.

The heavy knock sounded again, followed by raised voices.

Leo's heart thudded relentlessly in his ears. He turned and glanced at the door behind them.

"Come on," Jansons shouted, "we don't have much time."

The fist thumped against the door. The caller was getting impatient. Allissa glanced at Leo and then scrambled over the wall. Leo followed. They dropped down onto the flat roof. Gravel crunched beneath their shoes.

A thundering crack roared from the apartment behind them, and footsteps shuffled inside.

Leo bent double and pulled a deep breath of the humid air.

Jansons beckoned Leo and Allissa to follow him. Reaching the end of the flat roof, Jansons pointed down at the ground. There was still a good twelve feet to go. Jansons lowered himself from the edge and then dropped. He hit the ground and sunk expertly into a crouch.

Leo looked upwards and caught a glimpse of movement through the apartment's darkened windows. He pulled a deep breath and willed his muscles into action. The barbed wire of anxiety tightened further.

"Stop, do not move!" came a raised voice from the direction of the balcony. Leo turned slowly.

A man stood on the balcony. He was slight, muscular, and dressed completely in black. His eyes, like the twin barrels of a shotgun, were fixed on Leo and Allissa. He raised a gun.

Leo's stomach turned to iron. His legs froze like lead. His pulse thundered in his ears and he fought for breath.

No one could outrun a bullet.

## 50

"Put your hands in the air," the man shouted. He yelled some words in Latvian back into the apartment.

Leo tried to swallow. His throat was rough. He glanced at Allissa beside him. From somewhere far below, he heard Jansons' voice.

"Jump on the count of three. Trust me on this."

Leo looked at Allissa again. She nodded almost imperceptibly.

"One," Jansons said. His voice was nothing more than a hiss on the breeze.

The man on the balcony shouted in Latvian again. Another man appeared beside him. This man was large, with a shaved head. He also held a gun.

"Stay right where you are. If you move, you will be shot."

"Two," Jansons hissed again.

"If you move, you will be shot," the man repeated. "That would be bad for everyone. Especially you."

"Three."

An explosion roared from inside the apartment. The

windows flashed bright white. Glass shattered. Thick smoke billowed through the door and windows. The men on the balcony dropped their weapons to cover their ears. They stumbled backwards and gazed around in disorientation.

Leo and Allissa leapt backwards from the roof. The ground rushed up to meet them. Leo landed heavily on the grass. The fall sent a shock wave through his body and the breath lurched from his lungs. He rolled over and wheezed.

Leo and Allissa sprawled backwards. Leo gasped for breath. His legs and back ached from the landing. He examined his body. He didn't think he'd broken anything. The rucksack containing the documents was still looped around his shoulders.

"Come on, get up," Jansons shouted. "We must go. We do not have much time."

Leo and Allissa scrambled to their feet. The explosion's reverberations died out and ringing pounded in their ears. Leo glanced over his shoulder. Smoke poured in great clouds from the windows of the apartment.

"This way!" Jansons led them around the corner of the building and across to a small car park. Leo forced the fresh air into his lungs and attempted to slow his breathing. He needed to stay focused now. The barbed wire of anxiety loosened slightly.

Jansons led them towards a group of four cars, two dark-coloured hatchbacks, an SUV and a white Mercedes that must have been thirty years old. None of these escape vehicles filled Leo with hope. Jansons made a beeline for the Mercedes. Leo's sense of foreboding grew.

Jansons pulled a set of keys from his pocket and lunged for the driver's door. He yanked the door open, got in, then leaned over and opened the passenger door and the doors in the back. Leo and Allissa reached the car a moment later.

They piled into the back and slammed the doors. Despite its age, the car was in pristine condition. The leather upholstery, in dark brown, still had its sheen, and the carpets were spotless.

Jansons slid the key into the ignition. The engine clunked and whirred and died. Jansons muttered a string of Latvian expletives.

Leo caught Allissa's eye. His heart pounded in his chest.

Jansons turned the key again. The engine clunked, whirred, sputtered a little and died. He reached beneath the steering wheel and pumped a lever several times.

Leo looked back at the apartment block, twenty yards away.

"Urm, Jansons," Leo said, pointing in the direction of the building behind them. More specifically, pointing at the three men who were now charging towards them. One of the men dropped to one knee and levelled his weapon at the car.

"What? Hold on," Jansons barked, cranking the ignition again. The engine sputtered. This time the car shook, but still the engine failed to start. Jansons pumped the lever again.

"But, Jansons —" Leo said between gasps, his anxiety on full alert.

"Don't worry, this beauty has never let me down." Jansons cranked the ignition again. The engine groaned and coughed. A cloud of black smoke belched from the exhaust.

Leo's eyes were fixed on the men, now less than fifteen yards away.

"Jansons, the men! We need to go now."

Jansons glanced in the rear-view mirror and swore again. "Okay, okay."

The two larger men stopped running and levelled their

weapons at the car. No shots had yet been fired, but the car was now flanked on two sides. The smaller man, the one who had spoken on the balcony, charged on.

"Come on, come on," Jansons muttered. He looked skywards and touched his chest. He twisted the key. The engine whirred and crunched. The whizzing increased in pitch like a dynamo. More black smoke belched out.

Leo glanced from the window. The running man was just feet away now.

Jansons floored the accelerator and finally, not a moment too soon, the old car thumped into life. The engine roared. Jansons bellowed with laughter and slapped the steering wheel. He crunched the car into gear and hit the accelerator.

The pursuer, now just feet away, launched himself forwards. A dull thump pounded from the rear of the car. The man collided with the window and scrambled for a hold.

Jansons pushed harder on the accelerator. The tyres screamed against the crumbling tarmac and the ancient Mercedes lurched forwards.

The man grabbed onto the ridge where the boot connected with the roof.

Jansons gripped the steering wheel as the revs climbed. Leo glanced behind at the man, now lying across the rear windscreen.

The two other men traced the car with their weapons, searching for the shot, but not wanting to hit their colleague.

Jansons reached the road and spun the wheel to the left. The man slid across the rear windscreen, but somehow remained in place. Jansons hit the brakes. The man slid forwards. His grip held firm. The man climbed forwards and removed one of his hands, no doubt in an attempt to reach his firearm.

Jansons saw the movement in the rearview mirror. He floored the accelerator. The needles on the Mercedes' dashboard quivered up into the red. He swung the wheel hard to the right and thumped the brake. The car barrelled hard right. Leo and Allissa slid into each other on the back seat. Leo's head bounced off the glass.

The pressure was too much for the man. He flew from the car and rolled onto the grass beside the road.

Jansons didn't pause for a moment. He hammered the accelerator, and the car lurched forwards again.

The other men, seeing their colleague was out of the way, squeezed off several shots. They were now too far away for accuracy. Two lodged themselves in the bumper and the rest zipped wide.

Jansons stamped on the accelerator. They flew past large concrete buildings on both sides. Reaching the main road, they turned off into the anonymous traffic.

## 51

Vilis Mikhail watched the Mercedes tear away, swing violently to the left and join the main road. They were heading away from the city.

He struggled shakily up to his knees. He let the quivering of his vision subside and rose carefully to his feet. He looked down at his body.

A long gash ran down his left upper arm, and his hip throbbed. Being thrown clear of the road and landing on the grass was a stroke of luck. The only stroke of luck so far in this whole wretched job.

How that old guy detonated the smoke bombs and got out of the apartment was nothing short of ridiculous.

He glanced behind him and beckoned his men over. They holstered their weapons and walked across the grass. Vilis watched them approach. Both impending figures were built of equal parts muscle and attitude. They were efficient and deadly. The best Vilis had ever worked with.

"Why aren't we chasing them?" one of them said, stopping alongside Vilis. The Mercedes disappeared from view. "Your father's not going to be happy."

"Shut up," Vilis barked, snatching his phone from a pocket. "It's all under control." He unlocked the phone. He was relieved to see that it still worked. A map of Riga filled the screen. A blue dot drifted south on the A5. "What's the point in chasing them when we know where they're going."

## 52

"That was close," Allissa said, taking a deep breath as they accelerated past Zolitūde's concrete towers.

"Na, was fine!" Jansons replied, beaming in the rearview mirror. "This beauty got many years in her yet." Jansons worked a cigarette from the packet and jammed it between his lips.

"I'm not so sure," Allissa said, smiling back.

Leo clung on to the rear of the driver's seat, working to get his breathing under control.

"What happened to your stereo?" Allissa pointed to the hole in the dashboard where a stereo would normally go.

"Other than the starter motor and lights" — Jansons looked at her in the mirror — "this car has no electronics."

"Why?"

"Electronic equipment can be used by them. Look at that guy..." — Jansons pointed at a top of the range Porsche two cars ahead — "that car will have a tracker and an immobiliser built in. And the entertainment system will listen to what you're saying. That would be no good. They wouldn't even need to follow us."

Allissa nodded.

Leo finally got control of his breathing. His pulse slowed. He blinked hard. "What happened back there, with the explosion?" His voice sounded croaky.

Jansons waved Leo's concern away. "Oh, that's nothing. A couple of smoke bombs attached to a remote detonator of my own invention. They've been installed for years, but I've never needed them before. That reminds me." Jansons dug an old-fashioned mobile phone from his pocket and passed it back to Allissa. The thing was half the size and weight of a house brick. "Take the sim card out of that and throw it out of the window."

Allissa clicked off the back of the phone, slid out the sim card, wound down the window and flicked it out.

Silence descended over the car. Allissa wondered where Jansons was taking them. She watched him light up the cigarette and exhale a plume of smoke through the open window.

Some time later, as the sky was beginning to darken, Jansons pulled from the main road and onto a track lined by trees on both sides.

"No one will find us down here," he said, pulling the car to a stop in a layby. He killed the engine and slumped back in the seat. The engine gurgled into silence. Wind hissed through the tall pine trees.

Leo looked at the dense woodland through the window. Beneath the thick canopy of the trees, darkness was assembling in preparation for the evening ahead.

"I've never forgiven myself, you know," Jansons said, his eyes fixed on a point somewhere through the windscreen.

"What for?" Leo asked.

"For what happened to Emilija and her father. I helped Marija with her escape plan. I should have seen the flaw in the plan. But time was short. We had just days to arrange it, so we had to take risks that we wouldn't have normally. Somehow Mikhail found out." Jansons shook his head at the memory.

"The same Mikhail as...?" Allissa asked.

"Yes, the man who will probably be president in a month's time. He killed Peteris, Marija's husband, and Andreja and Emilija's father. And he probably killed Emilija too."

"And in a month's time he'll be the president. A murderer will be president?" Allissa looked out at the shivering trees.

"Yep. That's life, I suppose. The bad guy ends up leading the country while the good guy is on the run."

"That makes no sense," Leo said, shaking his head.

"No, that's not life," Allissa said, a serrated edge to her voice. "It doesn't have to be that way."

Jansons turned around in the driver's seat. His pale eyes moved slowly from Leo to Allissa. His expression was solemn. He cleared his throat.

"Listen, I've spent my whole life fighting this guy. I've tried every way I could think of to bring him down. I've tried to tell people about his past, but no one will listen. Nothing works. The more I've tried, the stronger he gets. I'm always the one who ends up with nothing." Jansons paused and rubbed a hand across his face. The trees swayed and hissed in a heavy gust of wind. "Five years ago, I tried to take him to court, and it nearly cost me everything. People just don't want to believe the truth about him. They're all walking around in some kind of daydream, listening to everything he says. I can't change the minds of a whole country. My life has been wasted on this." Jansons cuffed a tear from his face. "When you called and said you had this map, I saw a glimmer of hope, but now I see that was too much. They have taken Andreja, and they have taken any evidence she had. We don't even know where they've taken her. I have nothing. You should go now... don't waste your lives like I —"

"Hold on a second," Allissa said, interrupting Jansons' monologue. She placed her hand on his forearm. Jansons met her eye. "We said they had taken Andreja and ransacked her hotel room, sure. But we didn't say anything about them getting the map."

Jansons' jaw hung open. His mouth moved as though trying to speak. The words didn't come out.

"They've got Andreja, and ransacked her room, but they didn't find what they were looking for. Andreja was much cleverer than that." Leo lifted his bag from the foot-well, undid the clasp, and pulled out the folder.

Jansons beamed. "What? How? I don't understand. How did she do it?"

Leo and Allissa explained their visit to the left luggage place and the wine merchant. Jansons turned the folder in his hands as though it held magical powers.

When Leo and Allissa had finished, Jansons flipped open the lid and pulled out the wine-stained pages. Jansons examined each page in turn and placed them on the passenger seat. He looked through the whole pile and then pulled out three pages. He spread them across the dashboard and examined them closely.

For several minutes no one spoke. Beyond the windows, the sky bruised from orange to purple and then on to black. Jansons snapped on the cabin light so that he could continue working.

Eventually, he laid the three pages that were of particular interest to him across the dashboard.

"We tried comparing them to a road map already," Allissa said. "None of the lines match up —"

"To roads in Latvia anyway," Leo interrupted.

"To roads, yes," Jansons said. "But back then, for the work we did we didn't use roads. You see, these forests" — he pointed at the thick trees beyond the window — "well, they cover over forty percent of the country. During Soviet Union, the roads were patrolled, so we used tracks through the woods. Some were so small that they could only be followed on foot."

Leo and Allissa smiled with the realisation.

"And this is a map of those secret pathways?" Allissa said.

"Exactly," Jansons said, pointing a yellowed finger at Allissa.

"Can you tell where this secret file store is?" Leo asked hopefully.

Jansons snatched one of the pages from the windscreen and held it up. "Right there." He poked the page with his finger. "If this is what I think it is, it could tell us what happened to Emilija and bring down that bastard Mikhail."

## 53

Mikhail gazed out at central Riga through the window of his office. The sun had just struggled beneath the horizon, and night had settled uncomfortably across the city.

He examined the traffic below, streaming to and from the city. A blue and white tram rattled to a stop at an intersection. A group of people wearing shorts crossed the road and ambled in the direction of the park.

He brought the glass of scotch to his lips and sipped greedily. The liquid warmed his mouth and throat as it slipped inside. Mikhail exhaled and rolled his head from side to side. A knot of tension had started to form between his shoulder blades. Try as he might, he couldn't seem to shift it.

Mikhail cast his mind back. 1973 seemed like such a long time ago now. Surely, people wouldn't hold him responsible for things that happened so long ago. He looked down at the glass, the golden liquid shimmering. He needed to sort this, to silence it, before anything got out. There were enough people in this city who would love to see his career ruined.

Several stories below, the traffic light changed from green to red. The tram wheezed, purred, and then rumbled into life.

Mikhail had spent his whole life working for this city. Was it his fault that the opinions of the world had changed, now casting the things he did in a sinister light? He'd done what was required to keep the lights on, to keep soldiers from the streets, to keep food in the shops. No one could blame him for that.

He remembered that night again. 1973. They should have looked harder. They should have locked down the ports until Marija and the daughter had been found. But that would have taken an explanation. An explanation Mikhail hadn't wanted to give.

The Latvian forests in the winter were fatal. He knew that. Minus twenty at night. No one could have been expected to survive that, surely. Two frozen bodies would have been the ideal ending to a messy situation.

Mikhail's hand tightened around the glass. His lips twisted into a snarl. If he'd known the problems that woman and her godforsaken daughter would have caused, then he'd have searched the forest himself.

The shrill ringing of a phone pierced the silence. Mikhail crossed to his desk and snatched it up.

"Yes," he barked, slumping into his chair.

The only light in his office was a green shaded lamp on the desk. It cast an eerie glow up and around the room.

"They got away, but we're —" Vilis's voice sounded distant against the rumble of a moving vehicle.

Mikhail launched into a string of Latvian expletives. He slammed his glass down on the table. The golden liquid splashed onto the table's green leather inlay.

When Mikhail's anger had subsided, Vilis continued.

"We're following them. We have a tracker on their car. They'll lead us straight to whatever they have."

"Where are they now?" Mikhail's lips twisted in thought.

"Heading towards Dobelnieki. We're a few miles behind them."

"Okay." Mikhail's expression formed into a dark smile. "I'm coming too. Get someone to pick me up. This time I'm doing this properly."

## 54

Leo stared through the window as the ancient Mercedes wallowed through the impenetrable darkness. Walls of pine trees hemmed in the road on both sides. Above them, the sky was cloudless and star filled. The soft glow of the car's headlights cut about forty feet ahead before fading to nothing.

They passed a closed petrol station. The lights were off and metal shutters were drawn down against the evening. A sign on the forecourt spun lazily in the breeze. For a moment, Leo remembered the journey he and Allissa had taken through the mountains of Nepal. That taxi must have been a similar age to Jansons' Mercedes. The journey felt like a long time ago now. As the petrol station faded into the restless gloom, Leo tried to work out how long exactly. He couldn't really remember. In one sense it felt like a long time because so much had changed. In another, it felt like only last week.

Jansons lit a new cigarette from the butt of the last. He flicked the old one out of the window.

Leo glanced at Allissa sitting on the backseat beside

him. He slid his hand across the upholstery and placed it on top of hers. So much had changed in that time, and yet, here they were again, risking their lives for the right thing.

Jansons slowed the Mercedes and pulled to a stop at a junction. The brakes squealed and the car juddered.

Leo looked one way and then the other.

Strong headlights pierced the trees on the right. The deep grumble of a large engine carried through the silent night. Another vehicle was approaching. Leo glanced at Jansons. He showed no concern at the approaching vehicle. The lights grew in intensity until two trucks lurched from the darkness. Their giant loads of felled pine trees streamed through the ghostly glow of the Mercedes' headlights.

When the trucks had passed, their taillights already merging between the wisps of mist, Jansons pulled out into the intersection and turned right.

They drove in silence for several minutes. The temperature had dropped now, and strings of fog hung in the road's dips. It washed up over the windscreen, obscuring the view for a moment before the Mercedes reared upwards towards higher ground.

Jansons slowed the car and pulled onto the gravel at the side of the road. He snapped on the inside light. Colours danced in front of Leo's eyes. He blinked.

Jansons grabbed the three pages he'd separated from the others and looked at each one closely. He muttered to himself quietly, tracing lines from one page to the next. His cigarette bobbed in the corner of his mouth. Leo couldn't understand what he was saying. The engine of the Mercedes idled softly.

"We're close," Jansons said finally. He pointed through the rear windscreen. "It's been a long time since I've been here, but I know we're close." He lit a new cigarette, snapped off the light and accelerated away.

The Mercedes continued to sway down the undulating tarmac. The road was straight and featureless. Leo had no idea how long they'd been driving. He glanced at Allissa beside him, her eyes wide in the darkness. He turned and watched the dip and catch of an electricity cable running parallel to the road. Mist clung to the hollows beneath the trees, like an army preparing for attack.

Without warning, Jansons smashed on the brakes. The Mercedes squealed to a stop. Grit skittered across the road. Leo and Allissa jarred against their seatbelts. Jansons fought the gearbox into reverse, turned, and placed his arm across the passenger seat. A broad smile lit his face. He reversed fifty yards back up the road.

"There we are," he said, pointing his cigarette at the tightly packed trees beside the road. "I told you we'd find it."

## 55

Leo squinted at the tightly-packed trees, washed in the pale light of the low-hanging moon. He couldn't see anything that resembled a track.

"I'll show you," Jansons said, when neither Leo nor Allissa replied. He clunked the old Mercedes into gear and flung the steering wheel hard to the right. The car bumped and vibrated down the bank and towards the wall of trees. For several moments, it appeared as though they were heading for a direct collision with one of the trunks.

The Mercedes' worn tyres slid and skittered on uneven ground. Leo gripped onto the door handle. Jansons accelerated through a low-lying wreath of mist. The grey, oily vapour slipped across the windscreen. Finally, Leo saw the gap in the trees to which Jansons was leading them.

The car barrelled sideways across the rutted track. Jansons pushed the accelerator harder. Something scraped and scratched against the chassis. Earth sprayed up the doors. Leo glanced up at the moon as it was swept beneath the trees' dense curtain. The night swallowed them whole.

The car swayed, then skidded, then settled into a consistent forward motion.

"It's lucky there's been no rain," Jansons said, peering out at the narrow track before them and raising his voice against the rattling car. "These tracks used to be impossible to drive on when it was wet. Many of them we just had to follow on foot. We had whole teams of people moving stuff around by the cover of these trees."

"You've been here before?" Allissa asked.

"I don't remember this particular track, no. But there are many, all over the country."

Leo leaned forward and stared through the windscreen. The track twisted ahead through the densely-packed trees. Mist clung to the hollows and occasional spears of moonlight battled their way through the canopy.

The track dropped down a gentle hill before crossing a stream. Jansons stopped the car and peered out at the road ahead. Many winters of heavy rain had cut a deep trench through the forest.

"We'll not get any further in this," Jansons said, crunching the car in reverse.

"How far is it now?" Leo asked, examining the road ahead. After the stream, the track rose sharply and turned out of sight.

"Not very far," Jansons replied. "I don't know exactly. These maps aren't detailed. We're going the right way, though. I know that for sure."

Jansons spun the wheel, and the Mercedes bounced from the track. He rounded three densely packed trees and stopped.

"We don't want to advertise that we're here." Jansons clambered out of the car and straightened up.

Leo and Allissa climbed out, too.

"You don't have to come. You can wait for us in the car if you like," Leo said, hoping the old man would agree.

"Absolutely not," Jansons said, walking around the car and opening the boot. "I've been waiting decades to find this place. And I'm going to find it." Jansons rummaged around and produced two torches. He passed one to Allissa. The torches must have been as old as the car.

Allissa turned it on and a thin, orange finger of light cut through the trees.

"Help me with this," Jansons said, pulling a thick blanket from the boot. "It's camouflage. It'll stop anyone seeing the car from the track."

"You really have thought of everything," Leo said, accepting one side of the cover and helping Jansons drape it across the car.

"Like I said, I've been preparing this for decades." Jansons beckoned Leo around to the boot and pointed at a camouflage rucksack. "Now grab that bag."

Leo picked up the bag. Something slid about inside.

"Wooah, be careful with it, though," Jansons said, helping Leo slip the bag across his shoulders. "It's got one or two of those smoke bombs in it."

The woodland was alive with sounds now. A light breeze murmured through the trees. Somewhere nearby an animal called out and darted away.

Jansons, Allissa and Leo picked their way towards the stream. They crossed the small trickle of water with ease on foot. In the weak light from the torches, Leo noticed that the stream had worn a hollow of several feet into the soft forest floor. The crossing may have been possible in a 4x4, but the Mercedes would never have made it.

Leo held out a hand to help Jansons across. The man

shook his head and leapt across the void with surprising speed and balance.

Halfway up the opposite bank, Leo turned and peered back through the forest. The Mercedes, behind the trees and beneath its camouflaged covering, was invisible.

"Keep up," Allissa hissed. Leo turned and hurried behind them.

They climbed for another hundred yards and the ground levelled out. The trees were less densely packed here, their outlines visible in the moon's pale light.

Allissa swept her torch across the ground before them. Several stumps punctuated the ground like stubble.

A distant rumble vibrated through the forest. The three stood rooted to the spot. Two hundred yards away, a light cut through the trees.

## 56

Mikhail peered out from the back of the Mercedes Benz G Class 4x4. Densely-packed trees lined both sides of the road. Slivers of mist cowered in the hollows as though too scared to come out into the open.

Mikhail ran a hand across the shape of his gun, hidden beneath his jacket. This was the right way to finish it. This whole escapade had started in a forest nearly fifty years ago. Now Mikhail was going to make sure it ended in a forest, too. He was going to make sure it ended in a way that left him free to rise to power.

Two men, part of Mikhail's personal security detail, sat in the front seats. They were armed, willing and discreet — everything Mikhail needed today.

A radio crackled, and Vilis's voice filled the car.

"We shouldn't be waiting like this. They're in the forest. Only four-hundred yards away. We should take them now."

Mikhail snarled and indicated that the man should pass him the radio.

"You'll do what you're told," he barked into the handset.

"If it wasn't for your idiocy, they would already have been dealt with. Stay where you are. We're three minutes out."

Silence down the line showed Vilis's acceptance.

The G Class pulled up at an intersection. Mikhail glanced out at the road. It stretched silent and empty into the swirling mist on either side.

Mikhail looked at the screen on the dashboard, which indicated the location of Vilis and his men. They were close now.

The driver turned to the right and accelerated quickly on the empty road. The 4x4's engine growled through the night. The strong headlights cut a path through the churning banks of dirty fog.

Something glimmered and shone in the distance. As they came closer, another identical Mercedes Benz G Class materialised on the side of the road. Its engine idled softly against the whispering trees.

Mikhail gave instructions, and they pulled up alongside. Mikhail slid down his window. In the back of the other vehicle, Vilis did the same.

"Where are they?" Mikhail growled.

"There's a small track, fifty yards ahead. It's not on our maps, but looks as though it leads deep into the forest. Four-hundred yards down and on the right."

Mikhail peered into the gloom. "Okay, follow us."

## 57

The light cut through the forest like a thin shard. Shadows danced and swept across the landscape. The *thump thump* of steel on steel vibrated through the empty landscape.

Leo saw distant shapes a few hundred yards ahead, lumbering from right to left.

"Freight train," Jansons hissed, pointing towards the sound. "There's a railway line." As though introducing itself, the train's horn issued a mournful shriek.

Jansons picked his way forward, carefully avoiding tree stumps. Leo and Allissa followed.

The weight of the bag on Leo's back reminded him of its contents. He really didn't want to fall over here.

They reached the railway lines as the final carriage of the freight train rumbled away. The locomotive was already growing small, its headlight now melting into the fog.

Jansons stepped up onto the tracks. Four sets of rails ran dead straight in either direction. The red light of a signal glowed a few hundred yards away. A strand of mist hung across the tracks.

They crossed the rails. The heavy *thud thud* of the receding train thundered through the steel. Leo thought about the last time he climbed across railway lines. That time he had been on Berlin's U-Bahn on the trail of a missing man.

"There," Jansons said, reaching the other side of the tracks. Leo and Allissa stopped dead and followed his gaze. A building stood a few hundred yards to their left. A giant stack of freshly-chopped trees were piled on one side and a tractor sat dormant on the other. All the building's windows were dark, and no smoke came from the chimney.

"How do you know that's not just someone's house?" Allissa asked doubtfully.

"The map said that it was just after the railway." Jansons scrambled down the embankment at the side of the tracks.

Leo glanced at the fading light of the train. In the distance, the sky was stained with light from the city.

"It's exactly the sort of place they'd use," Jansons said, crouching down beside the tracks and peering at the building. "There are hundreds of little cabins like this all over the country. Hiding in plain sight. They're normally used by the men who clear the forest."

"It doesn't look like anyone's there," Allissa said.

"Probably not. If the files are here, their location is protection enough. Men with guns would be noticed."

"Guns?" Leo said, his throat dry.

The train's horn echoed through the still night air. A large bird, disturbed by the noise, pounded away above the trees.

Leo's hands clenched into fists.

Jansons scurried across an open stretch of ground and crouched down beside a set of tyre prints. He beckoned Leo and Allissa towards him.

Leo's eyes darted around the pitch-dark woodland, searching for movement. Something rustled in the undergrowth. His heart thundered like the wheels of the train.

"These are the newest tracks here." Jansons illuminated a set of thick tyre tracks with his torch.

"How can you tell?" Allissa asked.

Leo stood behind Allissa, the bag hanging heavily on his back. He tried to slow his quickening breaths. Everywhere he looked, his mind's eye projected ghostly figures manifesting from the dense shadows.

"See how they cross the others." Jansons swept the torch across the ground. "They were made when the ground was wet. We haven't had rain in a week."

"That doesn't mean that someone didn't walk here, or they're not waiting inside," Leo said, struggling to keep the panic from his voice.

"I'll check." Jansons darted across to the building.

Leo and Allissa moved in close to the giant rusting wheels of an idle tractor. A set of giant spikes protruding from a mechanical arm on the front of the machine glinted menacingly.

Jansons reached the nearest window and peered in. He cupped a hand above his eyes and shone his torch through the glass. He turned back to face Leo and Allissa, then shook his head. He darted around the other side of the building. He appeared again and beckoned Leo and Allissa over.

"All empty," Jansons said, barely above a whisper. "It doesn't look like anyone's been in there for a while."

Leo was not reassured by his whispering. If no one was nearby, why bother?

Leo glanced around again. A thickening cloud of mist

now swarmed towards them, turning the red signal light into a deep orb.

"Okay," Allissa said. "Cameras?"

"Couldn't see anything." Jansons swept the beam of his torch around the door. The cabin was a crude construction of wood and sheet metal. "But I don't suggest we stay around that long. There could be alarms or something. We get in, get what we need, then we get out of here."

"Agreed," Leo said, a shiver working its way up his spine.

"How do we get in?" Allissa said.

"Don't you worry about that." Jansons turned and smiled at them in the torchlight. He stepped up to the door. "A door like this never stopped a locksmith. Come here and hold the light." He beckoned Allissa across and pulled a small set of tools from his jacket. The tools scraped and crunched their way inside the lock. Jansons lowered into a crouch and twisted the lock. The mechanism clicked, and the door swung open. The ancient hinges groaned.

"You're a useful guy to have around," Allissa whispered, sweeping the room with the beam of her torch.

"Wasted youth," Jansons replied.

Leo glanced back at the woodland. Something crashed and scurried through the undergrowth. A bird hooted. He watched Jansons and Allissa step inside the cabin. The coil of barbed wire knotted tighter around his heart.

Allissa's eyes followed the weak beam of the torch as it swept around the cabin's interior. The walls and floor were constructed from rough wood. The ceiling was sheet metal supported by large wooden beams. Allissa could tell from the pitch of the roof that this room occupied half the building's space.

"We used to rely on these places all the time. There was a whole network of them." Jansons' voice took on the warm tones of nostalgia. His torch beam roamed from the stone fireplace and chimney-breast that occupied one wall, to two metal chairs covered in cobwebs.

"We'd travel only at night and sleep during the day. Only one person would know the route. I don't think I ever came to this one, though."

Allissa imagined what that would be like, sheltering in a place like this, not knowing what you were going to face the next day.

Jansons pushed against the door in the dividing wall. It didn't move.

"That's interesting." He cast a glance at Leo and Allissa. Excitement sparkled in his eyes. "Why would this door be locked?"

Jansons dropped to his knees and removed his tools. Allissa stepped forwards and shone her torch on the lock.

"That's a serious lock for an internal room," Jansons muttered. His tools scraped and clicked against the mechanism. Jansons frowned in concentration and leaned closer. Finally, after several minutes' effort, the lock disengaged, and the door swung open.

"Steel." Jansons tapped the door. The metal clanged loud in the quiet room.

Allissa followed Jansons inside. The bare walls and floor were constructed of the same rough wood. Three of the room's walls were lined with shelves. They ran from the floor, right up to the ceiling.

Allissa swept her torch across them. Her jaw fell open.

"What the —"

"If this is where the files were kept," Leo said, joining Allissa in the doorway, "why's there nothing here?"

Jansons' rough voice filled the empty room. "I think I know."

## 58

Mikhail's G Class bounced and wallowed down the rutted forest track. The engine grumbled and growled in the enclosed space.

The driver, experienced in the ways of the Latvian countryside, picked his way deeper into the gloom. The headlights sliced forward, disappearing to nothing amid the trees.

"One hundred yards on the right," came Vilis's voice, squeaking through the radio.

Mikhail glanced through the rear windscreen. Vilis's 4x4 was springing down the track behind them.

The Mercedes pitched down as the track descended into a valley. Mikhail peered through the windscreen. At the base of the valley, a small river came into view.

"Right, now," Vilis's voice came through the radio again. The driver obeyed, swinging the 4x4 from the road and out between the pines. He slowed the pace even further to pick his way between the trees.

"There, I see something," the driver said, pointing a thick finger in the direction of a clump of trees.

Mikhail squinted. The driver snapped on the 4x4's roof-mounted lights. Suddenly, the forest was awash with light. Sure enough, there was something there. Something glinted from behind the trees.

The other G Class pulled up alongside.

Mikhail got out and strode towards the trees. The other men followed.

Behind the guttural thump of the Mercedes' engines, the forest was silent.

"This guy is very prepared," Mikhail said, realising what was concealed there. A thick blanket, printed in shades of forest camouflage, was draped over the car. One exposed wheel trim had given the game away.

Mikhail grabbed the corner of the blanket and tugged it from the car. The white Mercedes shone beneath the 4x4's bright lights.

"Not prepared enough," Vilis said, sliding the magnetic tracking device from the roof, switching it off, and stashing it away. Mikhail glanced at his son. A fission of anger swept through him. If Vilis had done a proper job in the first place, then Mikhail would be at home right now. Mikhail should have left this sort of work to someone else a long time ago.

Vilis pulled open the door and made a quick search of the vehicle. "Nothing there," he said. "They can't have gone far on foot, though." He examined the forest's dry floor. There was no sign of any tracks. "We'll go one way, you go the other."

Mikhail turned and considered the smaller man.

"Think about this. Why would they have abandoned the car here?" He pointed in the direction of the stream. "Follow us."

## 59

Jansons' torch swept into the room and illuminated something in the far corner.

"Towards the end of the occupation they decided it was a liability to keep records in paper form," Jansons explained. "They could fall into the wrong hands very easily that way. Much research was done to find a way to store them electronically. It's rumoured that people still loyal to the old ways were trying long after the fall of the Union."

In the bead of light from Jansons' torch sat an ancient computer. The large, bulbous screen showed a distorted reflection of the room. The plastic casing was yellowed with age. The brains of the computer — the part that contained the processor and the all-important data — was mounted in a rack beside.

"It's all very impressive," Jansons said. "But, I'm afraid I know nothing about these machines." He took a step forward and looked closely at the screen. "How old do you think it is?"

"About twenty years," Allissa said, examining the dust

covered keyboard. "I remember using something like this back in school."

"Excellent. Then you'll be able to sort it, no problem," Jansons said.

Leo slid the bag containing Jansons' explosives from his back with relief. It was both heavy and having it close by made him nervous. He put the bag onto an empty shelf at the far side of the room and crossed towards the computer.

Allissa stooped into a crouch and examined the machine. Several modules sat behind a layer of filth.

"We're definitely going to need some power to get this thing going. Any ideas?"

Leo moved over to a light switch and clicked it on. No light appeared.

"There must be a central breaker," Leo said. "That maybe off, or maybe the place isn't connected at all."

"I'll look in here," Jansons said, pointing at the other room.

Leo searched the walls in the backroom. He looked between the shelves and beneath the desks. Nothing. He pulled an empty filing cabinet to one side and grinned.

"I think I've found something."

A chunky metal box was attached to the wall with thick cables running down into the floor. Leo couldn't see it clearly in the gloom.

Jansons hurried through and shone his light on the box. "That looks about right," he said, leaning towards the box. He yanked open a panel and hinges screamed. He thumped the switches inside. The fluorescent light on the ceiling buzzed, flickered, then burst into life.

The computer system whirred and buzzed. "We've got life," Allissa said, climbing to her feet.

Dull colours flashed on the screen. The colours grew in

intensity until a logo was legible. It wasn't a logo Allissa recognised. The logo faded, and a system prompted for a password.

"Any ideas?" Allissa asked Jansons. Jansons suggested several, but none worked.

"No problem, I think I can sort this," Allissa said, glancing at Leo. "I told you that boring course might come in useful."

Allissa's fingers flashed across the keys. The keyboard rattled. A blue screen appeared and Allissa adeptly scrolled through various menus and settings. The computer sprung to life.

"We're in," Allissa said, glancing at the men standing behind her. "These old models are much easier to crack. No up-to-date security."

"What do we do now?" Jansons said.

"Well, if we had time, I could run a search now. But we're probably just better to take a copy and search later when we're out of here." Allissa removed a flash drive from her key ring.

"Good idea," Leo said, his anxiety growing with each moment.

"This will definitely be everything you need?" Jansons asked, looking suspiciously at the small flash drive.

"I can't say for sure until we've looked through it. There's no telling what these files say about Emilija or Mikhail until we've searched them thoroughly."

"Could you just open one to make sure?" Jansons asked.

"It'll slow us down. Copying while it loads might push this dinosaur over the edge." Allissa pointed at the computer.

"Copy it and let's get out —" Leo's voice shook.

"We need to be sure," Jansons said, stepping forward.

There was a hard edge to his voice. "Open something, anything. I'll be able to tell if it was the sort of data kept in these files."

Allissa glanced from Jansons to Leo, and back to Jansons. "Okay, I'll do it."

She tapped the keyboard several times, and a file started to load. It loaded from the top and appeared in increments. An official logo appeared first. Then some writing appeared. Allissa assumed it was in Latvian.

Jansons leaned in and examined the screen. His hands gripped the table-top. His papery skin blanched of colour.

"It's an arrest report!" he shouted excitedly. "I don't know who it is, but that's good news. That's good news! We've done it." He grabbed Allissa's shoulder and bounced with excitement. Jansons rushed over to Leo and seized him by his shoulders too. "We've done it! We've found it!" he repeated, his face contorted into an ear-to-ear grin.

Allissa slotted the flash drive into a port on the front of the computer. Her fingers danced across the keys again. A loading bar appeared.

"We're copying," she said, sitting back.

"How long will it take?" Leo asked, trying to keep his voice steady.

Jansons released Leo's shoulders and paced around the room.

The computer clunked and groaned as the antiquated hard drives gave up their secrets.

"Six minutes and something," Allissa said. "Lucky they bought such a top of the range machine whenever this was done, otherwise we'd have no hope."

Jansons paused by the door. His eyes darted around the room. "Wait, wait!" he said, suddenly alert. "What's that noise?"

"It's the hard drive of this old thing." Allissa pointed at the computer. "I don't imagine it's been turned on in a long —"

"No, no, it's not that." Jansons charged back into the front room.

Allissa and Leo exchanged glances. Allissa surged to her feet and ran after Jansons. Leo followed. In the cabin's front room, another sound could be heard. Allissa listened closely. It was distant. But it hadn't been there before. Allissa glanced at Jansons, and then at Leo.

All three of them knew without doubt what they'd heard. The sound of an engine drifted through the still night air.

## 60

Mikhail peered out the rear window of the Mercedes G Class. Fifty yards behind, the other vehicle picked its way across the stream and scrambled up the bank. Dirt and fallen leaves shot out behind the wheels as Vilis accelerated too hard. The vehicle slid to the right and then to the left.

Mikhail sneered. That was the problem with Vilis. He was always in such a rush that he never thought things through. Sometimes getting something done wasn't about absolute power, but about subtlety and tactics. In that regard, Vilis still had a lot to learn.

Mikhail's 4x4 crested the hill, and the driver slowed to a crawl. The tree cover was less dense here. Large areas of forest had been cleared. The stubble of cut trunks and fallen branches littered the track on both sides. The moon hung low and ripe, bathing the eerie landscape in soft light.

Mikhail wound down the window and scanned the scene carefully. Other than the purring engine and the crunch of the tyres over leaves, the forest was silent.

"What's that?" Mikhail said, pointing to the left. A

distant red light streamed through the forest. "Dim the lights."

The driver snapped a switch and the 4x4's lights dimmed to a wraithlike glow. All three men in the 4x4 squinted at the light. Their question was answered by the sorrowful cry of a train's whistle.

"Railway," the driver said. "Dead ahead."

Mikhail nodded and rubbed his hands together.

"Slowly," he barked into the radio. "There's a railway line up ahead. We're crossing."

They approached the train line and paused. Four sets of tracks shone in the 4x4's low lights. Three heads twisted one way and then the other. To the right, a pin-prick of light was the only sign of the disappearing train. To the left, the signal glowed an angry red.

"Go," Mikhail said, "slowly."

The driver accelerated smoothly. They bounced over the first set of tracks. Shingle cracked beneath the tyres. The 4x4 lurched from side to side, rattling and banging. Mikhail held onto the door handle to prevent himself being thrown around in the back.

The driver's head flicked again from left to right, checking the tracks were still empty.

The front wheels rose again, up and over the next set of tracks. Gravel skittered from out beneath the rear tyres. They jarred back down.

A dog whined and barked from the back of the vehicle. Mikhail smiled at the sound. He turned to watch Vilis follow them up and on to the first set of tracks.

They crossed the final line and rolled slowly down the embankment. The driver stopped the 4x4. The engine growled softly.

Mikhail scrutinised the darkness. A smile broke across his face.

"There, look," Mikhail he said, pointing to the left.

A few hundred yards away, a wooden building was set against the wall of trees. It was nothing surprising. Used by the men who managed the woodland, there were countless similar places in the Latvian forests. This one was different, though. A light burned in one of the windows.

Mikhail's lips formed something of a snarl. He picked up the radio and gave instructions.

## 61

"Turn that light off now!" Jansons shouted. Leo sprinted back into the back room and killed the light.

"How long left on the copy?" Leo said.

Allissa checked the loading bar. "Four minutes."

Jansons and Leo stood at the window. Both watched the distant sweep of headlights through the trees.

"Vehicles, coming this way," Jansons yelled. "They must be four-by-fours to be coming from that direction. They're a couple of minutes off. Grab me the bag."

Leo did what Jansons asked.

The old man placed the bag on one of the metal chairs and tore open the zip. "Come here, see this." He dug through the bag. "There are two of these in here. I made them. Very good quality, you saw what they can do."

Jansons shone his torch at the device. It was a cylinder about six inches in length and three inches across. "These are set on a timer. You turn this, see here." Jansons demonstrated with a dial on one end of the device. "That side is about two hours, this side is about two minutes. Set and then make sure you're not nearby."

The sound of the engines droned more loudly now. There were at least two of them rising and falling in awful harmony.

"How long?" Leo hissed.

"Just over two minutes," Allissa replied.

"Yes. There isn't time. I'm going to lock you in that back room. I'll keep one of these in here with me. I'll keep the men distracted. You take the other. Use it to destroy the computer. Then find a way out of here."

"We've got time." Leo said. "We'll all be able to get out of here."

"No," Jansons said, his face now serious. "You stand a much better chance on your own."

"One minute!" Allissa shouted.

The noise of the approaching engines rattled louder. The ill-fitting windowpanes shook. Headlights cut through the grimy glass.

"We can do this. We can get away," Allissa shouted. "All of us —"

"No." Jansons zipped the bag up and forced Leo to take it. "Get back in there now. I need to lock you in. Use this to destroy the computer if you can. It's important you have the only copy."

Jansons shoved Leo backwards and swung the door closed. The steel thumped shut against its frame. Jansons' tools scraped in the lock for a few seconds, and the mechanism engaged.

Leo turned. His heartbeat hammered in her ears.

Tyres scraped against the loose ground as the first of the 4x4s pulled to a stop. Dust and earth spattered the front of the building. The first engine settled to an idle murmur.

"Thirty seconds," Allissa whispered, leaning over the computer.

Leo stared at the steel door. His hands hung limp at his sides.

The noise of the second 4x4 pulling up outside hammered through the walls. Both engines died. Car doors clunked open and heavy boots thumped across the ground.

"Fifteen seconds," Allissa hissed, looking from Leo to the computer screen and back again. "We need to get out of here."

The rusting hinges of the cabin's front door groaned. Heavy boots thumped against the cabin's floor.

"Ten seconds, we're almost there."

"I'm going to look for a way out," Leo whispered.

"Mikhail," came Jansons' voice through the dividing wall, followed by a sentence Allissa didn't understand. Another man replied, the one she assumed to be Mikhail.

The computer beeped quietly. The status bar disappeared from the screen. The copy was complete.

The voices raised into a shout. Someone thumped against the wall. Allissa imagined Jansons being pushed against the rough wood by one of Mikhail's men. She forced the thought from her mind. They had to get out now.

"There're no windows," Leo said, standing at her side again, "but I can see the light coming through the roof up there. I think one of the panels must be loose. I bet we can force it up and climb out."

"Good idea." Allissa hitched the bag up onto her back.

"Jansons said to use that to destroy the computer." Leo pointed at the bag.

"I've got a better idea. I can wipe the data manually. You never know, this might be useful later." Allissa glanced at Leo, fire in her eyes.

Mikhail shouted. Another thump shook the wall.

Allissa pulled the flash drive from the computer and looked at it. She wondered if this could really contain information so explosive that it could bring down a government? She didn't know for sure, but Jansons certainly thought so.

The metallic crunch of a weapon being loaded cut through the voices now. Mikhail shouted again.

Jansons was silent. Allissa imagined him smiling up at the other man, adamant that he would not give in. Although they'd only met a few hours ago, Allissa knew that Jansons was a tough bastard. They needed to be tough now too, to make sure justice was served.

Allissa sat down at the computer. Her hands flew over the keys. She needed to corrupt the data before they left. If these files were as important as Jansons suspected, there was no way Allissa could let them fall into the wrong hands.

Behind her, Leo climbed up the shelves to where the corrugated iron roof met the top of the walls. A crack of light shone through. Leo pushed gently on the metal. Sure enough, it moved. It must have come loose in a storm.

He pushed it again. The metal screeched and clanged.

Leo froze. That would immediately give their position away. If the men saw them escape, their path would be blocked.

Leo waited, breathing heavily.

A dull thud reverberated through the cabin. Leo imagined Jansons falling to the floor. Using the sound to disguise his movement, Leo pushed the corrugated metal with all his might. It groaned and clanged. The metal bent but didn't come loose. Leo swore. He wedged his shoulder against the weakest part and waited.

He hadn't expected the next sound. A gunshot rang out through the cabin, followed by a cry of searing pain.

Leo pushed as hard as he could, his face set in an expression of tension. Each muscle strained. The sheet metal bent, twisted and came loose. The fresh air of the evening lashed his face. Leo took a deep breath of it.

Leo gripped the loose section of the sheet metal and placed it to the side. He scrambled out of the gap and stood tentatively on the roof. It was about twenty feet above the ground. To his left, the wood pile created an easy descent to the ground below.

"Come on," Leo muttered, peering back inside. Allissa tapped ferociously on the computer.

"I'm out," he hissed as loud as he dared. "We need to go now."

Allissa glanced over her shoulder. "One minute," she mouthed silently.

Leo swallowed. His stomach tensed. A lot could happen in one minute.

Since they'd been inside, the mist had intensified. The cabin was now shrouded, reducing the shivering pines to ghostly brown brushstrokes.

Another gunshot roared from the room next door. Jansons cried out in pain.

A fist pounded on the connecting door. It struck three times and then stopped. When it returned, it was the barge of a shoulder.

Leo swore, then peered inside. With each strike, the door shook on its fittings.

The thumping intensified. Two men were now shouldering the door.

Allissa glanced from the screen to the vibrating door just a few feet away. She was so close. She just needed to make sure the program would corrupt the data on the hard drives.

She couldn't leave anything for these guys. If they could recover the data, it would all be for nothing.

The banging increased in volume and ferocity. The steel door was now buckling. It wouldn't last much longer against this tirade.

Allissa examined the details of the disk formatting operation on the screen. She made one last check to make sure everything was correct.

*Yes.*

She punched the return key and sprung to her feet. She took three steps across the room.

Leo watched from the roof space, his mouth a grim line of determination.

Another thump wobbled the thick steel door. Dust sprung from the dividing wall.

Allissa glanced back at the screen. A dialogue box sprung from the hazy pixels.

"Come on," she muttered. She turned and ran back to the computer.

*Y/N* was followed by a line of text in a language she couldn't read.

Crossing her fingers, Allissa thumped the Y key. The screen went dark.

She charged across the room and scrambled up the shelves.

The doorframe was away from the wall now. The men pounded again. The door shot further forwards. The screech of splitting wood filled the air.

Allissa climbed to the top shelf and poked her head through the hole.

Leo grabbed her arms and yanked her through. They both fell backwards, smashing into the metal.

The door fell inwards, clanging to the floor. Heavy boots

stomped into the room. Raised voices shouted Latvian words.

Leo and Allissa lay still for a few moments. The mist hung thick and heavy around them, as though it too was waiting for something to happen. A deep scraping noise reverberated from the cabin.

"They're moving the door out of the way," Leo whispered. "Follow me."

Leo scrambled to his feet and clambered on to the woodpile. The felled logs were secure beneath his feet. He pulled the backpack on tightly, a shard of worry striking his heart when he remembered the explosives inside.

He helped Allissa down beside him. Together they scrambled down to solid ground. Leo glanced over his shoulder and pulled them in the direction of the dense woodland.

"Wait, wait," Allissa said, her eyes wide. "We have to see what happened to Jansons."

"We can't go back, we have to —"

But Allissa had already scurried over and was standing against the wall of the cabin.

Leo swore under his breath and followed her. Their backs bent, they moved along the wall until they were beneath the window. Slowly, carefully, each stood up. The inside of the cabin was brightly lit, a square of balmy light shooting outwards.

Jansons lay on the floor, his shoulders up against the wall. Blood pooled on the surrounding floor. One of his arms was stretched out on the ground before him, the other was curled behind his back. Three men stood in the room. Leo imagined two more searching the back room.

Two of the men wore dark clothes with no sign of military rank or other insignia. Private guns for hire, Leo assumed. They stood with their backs to Leo and Allissa, cradling semi-automatic weapons. The third wore a well-made suit and a long overcoat. His grey hair was neatly styled, and a gold watch glimmered from his wrist.

"That's Mikhail," Allissa whispered. "He's the guy that —"

Mikhail barked something at Jansons.

Jansons spat a torrent of Latvian expletives.

Mikhail laughed out loud, his head tilting towards the sky. From beneath his coat he removed a gun and levelled it at Jansons' head.

Jansons smiled up at the other man.

Mikhail's stare intensified.

"We need to get out of here," Leo whispered. "Look… Jansons' arm." At first, Leo assumed Jansons had fallen on the arm, but now he realised what the man was doing in his last moments of life.

"No, wait, wait —" Allissa said.

"It's the explosive, the —"

At that moment, a smile crept onto Jansons' face. He pulled the cylinder from behind his back.

"You always were a bastard, Mikhail," Jansons said, flinging the device across the floor.

Mikhail's eyes burned. The gun wavered.

Leo pushed Allissa down to the ground.

Two gunshots echoed through the night.

Leo and Allissa scampered and crawled back behind the wood pile.

Raised voices and pounding footsteps carried on the night air.

The explosion ripped through the cabin. It reverberated out into the woods, bouncing from the trees and up into the night sky. Glass shattered. The cabin's roof clanged and crunched.

Footsteps clattered down the steps as the men fled back towards their vehicles. Voices were raised in fear.

Mikhail reached the nearest 4x4 and leapt behind it. One of the black-clad men followed.

Light filled the forest.

Leo and Allissa covered their ears and clamped their eyes shut. They rolled further behind the wood pile.

The sound followed. It ripped, roared and reverberated through the woodland for long moments. It thundered back and forth amid the trees. Something thumped, rattled and died. All went quiet.

## 62

Leo opened his eyes and glanced back at the cabin. Despite covering his ears, the explosion's distant hum rung through his skull.

He remembered what Jansons had said about the explosive devices. They weren't designed to kill anyone, just confuse them with light and sound.

A pair of torches clicked on from behind one of the 4x4s. Two men struggled to their feet and looked around in disorientation. Leo recognised Mikhail as one of them. Mikhail brushed down his suit and spat on the floor. He shouted commands at the other men. Two more men struggled to their feet and looked around, equally confused. Two torch beams appeared.

"I think it's time for us to go," Leo whispered. Allissa nodded.

Keeping the wood pile between them and the men, Leo and Allissa crawled away from the cabin. Torch beams swept the woodland all around them. Leo listened closely, expecting at any moment to hear raised voices and running feet. They never came. Mist swirled around them.

Leo and Allissa reached a pair of trees and crawled out of sight. They peered out at the cabin now fifty feet behind. Mikhail lashed the men with words and pointed wildly. The confusion of the men started to shift. They looked around with more intensity. Two started searching the forest in the opposite direction. Mikhail gestured towards the 4x4s and shouted at no one in particular.

"Let's keep going," Allissa said, standing up. "I reckon we head away from the cabin for a few minutes and try to circle back towards the car."

Leo agreed. They stepped out into the darkness. Now away from the cabin, with the descending mist, the dark was absolute. The trees ahead of them glowed in the faint moonlight. Leo stumbled forwards on the uneven forest floor. His foot struck a fallen branch. He winced and swore. He reached out and held Allissa with one arm and extended the other in front of him to feel his way. He wished they'd brought one of the torches.

They picked their way forwards, step by step, inching through the forest. The whining in Leo's ears faded and a cacophony of forest sounds surrounded him. Something scuttled nearby. Leo glanced towards the sound, but saw nothing. The crunch of their footsteps and heavy breathing sounded like thunder. The trees hissed in the gentle wind. A bird cawed. The voice of a man rang from somewhere behind them. It now sounded a long way away.

Allissa stumbled over a fallen branch or uneven ground — it was impossible to tell. Leo wrapped his arm around her shoulder. They pushed on together.

"Wait, wait, let's stop," Allissa whispered. They turned and peered back in the direction of the cabin. Beyond the trees, the darkness and the thick mist, the place was now reduced to a soft glow.

"We can't keep going like this," Leo said, poking the surrounding ground with his toe. "We'll break an ankle or something."

"Or fall off a cliff," Allissa said sarcastically. She sounded very close. "Maybe they won't look this far," she said, peering into the gloom. "I can hardly see —"

But then a new sound resonated between the trees. It reverberated violently through the gloom.

"Did you hear that?" Allissa asked.

Leo nodded. The coil of barbed wire around his heart tightened even further.

## 63

Mikhail paced back into the cabin. Aside from the glass in the windows and two upturned chairs, the explosion hadn't caused too much damage.

The beam of his torch swept the room. He found a light switch beside the door and clicked it on. Nothing happened. The explosion must have broken that, too.

Vilis stepped into the room behind Mikhail, the beam of his torch also sweeping through the gloom.

Mikhail looked at the crumpled body on the floor. In the light of the torch, there was something creepy about him. The man lay at a funny angle. His arms and legs were splayed out on the wood around him. His head lay crooked, propped up against the wall. His pale eyes stared at the ceiling, motionless. Blood bloomed around three bullet holes in his chest and pooled on the floor. Jansons' heart had long since stopped beating, and the blood was now still.

"Did you really think you would be able to stop me?" Mikhail snarled in their native Latvian. He dropped into a crouch and met the lifeless stare.

The beam of Vilis's torch swept through the room behind him.

"I could have killed you years, no, decades ago. If you'd been anything more than an embarrassment to yourself, I would have done that. It had to end this way though, I suppose." Mikhail tapped the back of Jansons' hand. The body was cooling fast. "You in a shallow grave in the forest, me as president —"

"Come and see this," Vilis's voice boomed through the cabin.

Mikhail glanced up at the doorway. He pushed aside the irritation and climbed to his feet.

In the chaos of the explosion, Mikhail hadn't examined the cabin's back room.

He strode through the door, his torch illuminating the empty shelves. Vilis was bent over an ancient computer at the far end of the room.

"Do you know what this is?" Vilis said, glancing at his father.

"Yes," Mikhail replied, grinning. He swept his torch again around the shelves. "This is the most powerful store of information in our country. With this, no one could challenge me. Do you know how to make this work?" Mikhail pointed at the computer.

"Yes, I think so." Vilis replied, thumping some keys on the keyboard.

"Good. In that case, we have no use for our friends out there in the forest. Pass me your radio."

Vilis unclipped the radio from his belt and passed it to his father.

Mikhail's voice became deep and sonorous. "They are not to leave this forest alive."

## 64

Leo pulled Allissa closer as the sound of barking dogs thronged through the woods. There were at least two of them, growling and yapping as they barrelled across the forest floor.

Leo's heart leapt into his throat. The dogs were following their scent. The pitch-dark woodland offered no protection from a well-trained canine nose. The dogs would lead the men straight here.

The image of Mikhail pointing at Jansons flashed into Leo's mind.

His breathing became tight. He tried to pull a deep breath, but anxiety constricted his chest. His heart thundered.

"What should we do?" Leo asked, his voice wavering on the precipice of panic.

"Run," Allissa said. "Run, now."

Allissa set off, her arms outstretched, feeling her way forwards. Leo turned and ran, too. They kept their hands locked together until a tree forced them apart. Leo reached out for Allissa again, but she wasn't here. His feet thundered on, pounding over the uneven ground. Leo knew that he could run. He ran at home for exercise and to clear his mind. But not running like this. Not in an impossibly dark woodland, chased by dogs.

His pulse hammered against the wall of his chest. He paused for a second and turned. The barking had intensified. The dogs were closing in on their scent. There was another noise now, too. The voices of the men, following the dogs.

Leo glanced around. He saw a flicker of movement in the gloom. Allissa. Leo gave chase. Maybe they would reach a stream or lake or something — he'd read something about water diffusing the scent. Was that even true? Leo's feet pounded the ground. His breath laboured in his chest. The air was wet and cold. He pulled up alongside Allissa. He could just see her strained expression of panic in the moon's ghostly light.

They both paused again and listened. The growing chorus of their pursuers was close now. Leo stared into the dark forest. He willed his eyes to adjust further, to show him what horrors the gloom concealed. The snapping jaws. Slobber running from glinting teeth. Sharp claws propelling the snarling, vicious foe their way.

Another sound ground through the trees. Leo's head whipped towards it. A mixture of excitement, fear and now hope welled inside him. The sound came again. The loud, sorrowful screeching of a lumbering freight train.

Without exchanging a word, Leo and Allissa set off towards the sound with renewed energy.

The ground had levelled out here and their feet pounded softly across it. The forest's canopy was thinner too, giving them more milky light from the moon.

Leo's breathing dropped into sync with his thumping

feet. He took a long, deep breath of the forest air. He exhaled. Vapour billowed out before him.

The baleful cry of the horn sounded again. Now it was backed by the chuntering of wheels on steel.

Leo strained to listen for their pursuers, but nothing came. Maybe they were still some way off. He pushed harder, each step an explosion of energy driving him forwards. Jansons' backpack jolted left and right and on his shoulders. Leo had long forgotten the explosive power of the device inside. Now his whole focus was on each foot, hammering the ground with maximum power.

Allissa ran beside him, her hands pumping as fast as she was able. She gritted her teeth and attempted to keep up with Leo. Lactic acid burned her muscles like knives. With each aching step, she cursed herself for refusing to go running down the promenade in Brighton with him. That sedate and pleasurable run seemed like another world now. She glanced briefly over her shoulder. Was that movement she saw in the gloom?

The grinding of steel against steel was close now. Leo readjusted his direction and veered to the left. Allissa followed, gasping for breath. Her pulse roared like the nearby train.

Leo stumbled, and scrambled across a fallen tree. His feet slipped across rotten bark. He put his hands down and caught himself the moment before he fell. Allissa pulled herself over the tree behind him. They made the final few steps together and emerged, panting and frantic, from the woodland and onto the same four parallel railway lines they'd seen earlier. The lines cut a straight path through the forest. With the mist, hanging thick and dirty, the moonlight only lit a hundred yards in either direction. That was good. It meant the guys hunting them could only see that far too.

The barking of the dogs intensified. Their hunters weren't relying on sight alone. They must be getting close now.

To the left, a red signal glowed, refracting to a shapeless sphere through the fog. To the right, the single bright headlight of the incoming train pierced the night air. Brakes squealed and cars shunted as the train approached the red light.

"Get down," Allissa hissed, pulling them back behind a pile of fallen branches.

The locomotive passed. A giant machine, gurgling, rumbling and spitting a torrent of thick smoke into the air. Leo watched the driver, illuminated by the glow of the console. He hadn't noticed them. With an ear-splitting cacophony of screeching, the train came to a complete stop.

"This way." Leo pulled them down the track, away from the driver and the sound of the approaching dogs.

The train's wagons lay as far as Leo could see into the mist, still on the tracks like a massive dead snake. They hurried along the rails, hoping the driver was too occupied to see movement several feet below. The first few cars were cylindrical tanks. Graffiti scarred their curved bodies. Leo paused and glanced up at them. They would offer nowhere to hide.

He peered behind them. The red signal continued to glow. Their pursuers had yet to emerge. Leo and Allissa ran on.

Next came a series of empty flatbed cars. Leo swore. The drums of panic rose in his ears. Again, these would offer no protection. They would be seen instantly. He gazed up at the locomotive. It was invisible now, merged into the swirling fog.

A dog barked somewhere nearby.

Leo pulled Allissa further down the tracks. Gravel crunched beneath their feet.

Finally, a series of open wagons materialised from the mist. Leo recognised them as the sort used for carrying coal, or something like it.

Leo looked behind them as they crossed the two nearest lines.

The signal, just a distant glow, flicked from red to green.

"Quick, quick!" Leo shouted, pulling Allissa over the final empty train line.

A guttural roar emanated from the locomotive. A cloud of noxious smoke issued up into the air. The rails beneath their feet vibrated. Slowly, insidiously, the cars began to clunk and roll.

Leo reached the nearest car. The train was picking up speed but had yet to reach walking pace. He paused for a moment for the ladder at the far end of the car to approach him.

"Get up here," he shouted at Allissa two steps behind him. The train was picking up speed now. The heavy wheels groaned and growled along the rails. The couplings clunked and banged.

Allissa ran a few paces to catch up, and Leo stepped aside. She grabbed hold of the ladder and hoisted herself up. She scampered up the rungs and dropped down inside the car. Leo was jogging alongside the train now. The huge wheels screeched in protest as the locomotive picked up speed.

He took two long strides towards the ladder. What happened next occurred in a blur of movement. One moment, Leo was running towards the car, his hands destined to grasp the steel. The next, he was falling, his foot caught on something beside the rail. Leo saw it all in slow motion; the train moving, his arms reaching out for it. He fell against the gravel, arresting his fall at the last moment. Hot pain jarred through his wrist. The massive wheels of the freight cars rumbled along, just inches from his face. Leo's breath turned hot and heavy. He glanced down at his feet. His foot had fallen into a hole beside the track. He pulled it out and struggled back to his feet.

The train was picking up speed now. The *thump thump* of the rails merged into one constant shudder. Leo glanced up. Allissa watched him from the car twenty feet ahead.

"Run," she yelled, her voice carrying above the thundering train. "Now!"

Leo did as he was told. His feet found their grip on the uneven ground. He hammered alongside the train. He closed the first ten feet quickly, but then the train accelerated further. The locomotive slipped into a lower register, and the engine growled ominously.

Leo gritted his teeth and went into an all-out sprint. His feet surged into the rough ground as hard as he was able. The muscles in his chest ached. In a blur of movement and a flurry of pumping legs, Leo made it to the ladder. He grabbed hold of the cold steel and hoisted himself from the ground.

The train accelerated again. The ground rushed past beneath his feet. Leo pulled himself upwards, then rolled into the carriage beside Allissa.

Together they peered over the carriage's steel rim. The dense woodland slid alongside the track at increasing speed.

"Look," Allissa said, nodding towards a group of men beside the tracks. A pair of dogs yapped at their heels.

Leo took a deep breath, turned, and slumped down out of sight.

## 65

"Come look at this," Allissa said, peering over the side of the rumbling wagon.

For most of the journey, which he estimated to have lasted at least an hour, Leo had sprawled on the grit inside the wagon. His breathing had long since recovered, but his wrist and legs ached. Leo struggled to his feet and crunched across the gravel. The car lurched and shook. Leo stood next to Allissa, holding on to the thick steel side. The view lit his face with a smile.

The sky had warmed from a deep, inky black to a gradient of orange and purple. It was clear apart from a few clouds that hung low and plump, as though ready for harvest. Before them, the train snaked forward, its multicoloured cars visible in the coming light. A thick cloud of smoke bellowed upwards from the locomotive. A network of cables and pylons crisscrossed the sky in dark silhouettes. On the horizon before them, the dreamy spires and towers of downtown Riga clawed the heavens. Leo recognised the bulky spire of St Peteris's Church, the Sciences Academy Building, and further out of the city, the needle of Television

Tower. Then, as usual, when looking at something beautiful, he turned to Allissa.

Her skin glowed with the morning sun, and the excitement of the last few hours sparkled in her eyes. Leo leaned in and kissed her. A flurry of emotion passed through him. It was a new emotion. One he didn't yet understand. Ever since their first kiss, all those months ago, this feeling had smouldered deep inside him.

He glanced back at the skyline. A cool breeze whipped through the car, blowing Allissa's hair against him.

Mya. That was the last time he'd felt this way. But that was different. The way he'd felt about Mya had been darker, more oppressive and almost addictive. He likened it to the high of good drugs or the buzz of pure adrenaline. He just wanted more and would do anything he could to get it.

The way he felt about Allissa was different. It was instinctive and honest. A natural high, that had snuck inside him and lifted him up without warning. It was a sensation that, as yet, he didn't know how to verbalise. Rather, he knew exactly how to verbalise it, but he was afraid what that meant. He didn't know if it was reciprocated or if it was welcome. Things were good. Changing things could be disastrous. Last time Leo had tried that — with his proposal to Mya — she'd disappeared into Koh Tao's menacing night.

The high-pitched squeal of the brakes knocked Leo from his reverie. The cars clunked and clanged together as they slowed. Leo peered ahead. They approached a red light on their way into the city.

"I think it's time we got out of here," Allissa said, moving over towards the ladder and pointing down the side of the embankment. There was a gap in the wire fence. "Look down there."

"Good idea." Leo shook all thoughts of emotion from his head and followed Allissa across to the side of the car.

Allissa peered out. No other trains were approaching, and there didn't seem to be anyone watching.

The freight train finally squealed to a stop. The cars jarred backwards and forwards for a few moments before coming to rest. Allissa hopped over the side of the car and shimmied down the ladder. Leo followed as quickly as he could. Then, before anyone could see them, they hustled down the embankment and through the gap in the fence.

## 66

Normally frequented by drunks and philanderers, the Hotel Sigulda was basic in the extreme. Allissa opened the door and led them inside their room. The space was almost filled by the double bed in the centre.

"It's a shame we couldn't go back to the Esplanade," Allissa said, luxuriating in the memory of their previous hotel with its deep carpets, room service and whirlpool bath.

"I know, but that's exactly where they'll expect us to go." Leo placed Jansons' bag down with meticulous care and put the laptop they'd persuaded the receptionist to lend them on the bed. A night's rental of the decrepit computer had cost almost as much as it would to buy, Leo knew. Neither he nor Allissa had the energy to argue, though. Nor could they go back to the Esplanade Hotel to get their own laptops. So, Leo had exchanged a wad of slippery notes — pulled from an ATM on the other side of the city on the way there — in exchange for the use of the laptop for one night.

Allissa walked into the coffin-sized bathroom and

clicked on the shower. An almighty rattle issued from the pipes as a torrent of hot water, and then cold, and then hot again spurted out. Allissa let it run and filled up the kettle.

Leo plugged in the computer — the thing was so old the battery didn't work — and started it up.

After the computer had chugged to life and they'd both had tepid showers, Allissa pushed the flash drive into the computer's only port.

"Looks like it's worked," Allissa said as the file appeared on the screen.

Leo nodded, sipped his coffee, and cradled his aching wrist.

For half an hour they navigated through the files, picking them out almost at random and reading the contents. Allissa ran an online search for one of the names who'd been charged with a series of crimes in the 1970s. He was now one of the country's most prominent judges. Several recent articles quoted him from his speeches about his harsh stance against criminals.

"There's some explosive stuff here." Allissa finished off her coffee. The excitement of looking through the files had distracted her, and now it was cold.

"Yes, there is. But that's not what we're here for, remember. We need to stay focused. We're here to find out what happened to Emilija —"

"And where Andreja is," Allissa cut in.

"Yes, but I suspect they're linked somehow. If we start with Emilija, I think that'll somehow lead us to Andreja."

Allissa agreed with Leo's theory. She glanced at him and smiled. He cradled his wrist.

"What?" Leo said.

"Nothing. Just checking up on the wounded soldier." Allissa grinned.

"Just run a search for Emilija Panasenko." Leo waved his arm at the computer. He couldn't help but smile back.

"Nothing," Allissa said. "That's not surprising though, as the files are organised by date. And the files themselves are digital scans so they won't be searchable."

"Can we search by the year and month she disappeared?"

Allissa tried it. "Three hundred files. But, wait, I can get rid of loads of them because they're nothing to do with a child."

Leo nodded. Now they were getting somewhere.

Allissa clicked her tongue as she counted. Leo's grin broadened.

"That gets us down to twenty-five. Why are you looking at me like that?"

"Nothing, urrm, okay." Leo blushed and looked away. "I'll make some more coffee. Want some?"

Checking through the twenty-five scanned documents was agonisingly slow on the ancient computer. Especially considering they were in a mixture of Russian and Latvian, and many were written by hand. Using an online translator, Allissa reduced the list down to three. Three children had been re-homed in 1973.

"The name Emilija Panasenko isn't in this document either," Allissa said after she'd read the final one. Her spirits slumped.

"I don't think that matters," Leo replied. "If they were trying to hide her, I don't think they'd put her original name on there. Have you got access to birth records, too? I suspect one of those young girls wouldn't have a birth record and that would be —"

"Emilija," Allissa blurted out. "Yes of course."

Allissa noted down the dates of each girl's birth and

searched through the files. The first two she found easily. One had been born in Riga, the other in Ventspillis, both on the days detailed. The third was proving move difficult.

Allissa scanned through all the birth records for that day. Nothing matched. She glanced from the screen to Leo and back again. "I think we've got something," Allissa said. "Emilija was renamed after her family had escaped to England. She was called Zuza Milasa Salins."

## 67

Mikhail examined the city through the window of his office. The sun was still a few hours from its peak, and the day was already hot. Too hot, he decided, flicking a thumb beneath the top button of his collar and pulling it loose.

As Mikhail had expected from a presidential campaign, his morning had been manic. Back-to-back meetings and interviews on very little sleep had left him weary and more irritable than usual.

Then there was the man and woman who'd escaped last night. How they had done that, deep in the forests, several miles from anywhere, Mikhail had no idea. But the trail had just run cold — or so he'd been told. He fumed quietly, then took a sip of coffee.

What worried him, was that he didn't know anything about them. They had met Andreja Panasenko on the night she'd arrived. Then they'd been followed out to meet Jansons in Zolitūde. Then they'd just disappeared into the forest air.

It troubled Mikhail because he had no idea who they

were or what they wanted. They were currently a loose end. The last loose end Mikhail had let slip was Marija Panasenko, and that hadn't turned out well at all.

Whoever they were, they needed to be found, and they needed to be dealt with.

The phone on Mikhail's desk buzzed. He turned, then strode across to it and thumped the answer button.

"Vilis is here to see you," came his assistant's voice.

"Send him in and hold all my calls," Mikhail replied. "What have you got for me?" Mikhail said before Vilis had even stepped into the room.

Vilis crossed to the desk and sat down. "It's not good news, I'm afraid. The computer has somehow been corrupted."

"What do you mean, it's been corrupted? The information on there is essential!" Mikhail roared. He swung his arms wide in astonishment, knocking his coffee cup flying. It smashed against the wall. Mikhail swore.

"Everything on the hard drive is gibberish. It doesn't make any sense. I've had a team of experts working on it for the last five hours."

"How is that even possible? I know what that place was, and I know what information that system was supposed to hold."

"Yes, well, there's one thing that may interest you. There are certain fragments of information, apparently, that show the corruption happened very recently. Even as late as a few minutes before we got there."

Mikhail snarled. His hands gripped the table-top. He knew what this meant. He exhaled and looked closely at the coffee stain soaking into his office wall.

"Is there any sign of them?" Mikhail said.

Vilis shook his head. "My men are still searching the

forest, but it seems they just —" He spread his fingers and drew a circle in the air.

Mikhail rose to his feet and paced over to the window. There would be a time to get angry, but this wasn't it. Right now, he needed to be calm and focused. He would sort this, like he had sorted every other problem in his career.

"Tell me what we know about them," Mikhail snapped at Vilis.

Vilis ran through the details once again. Mikhail had heard them all before. Then something occurred to him.

"Zuza Milasa Salins," he muttered, his mind's eye imagining the distant forests on the horizon.

"Who?" Vilis said.

"I think I know why they're here, and if I'm right, I think I know where they'll go next. Listen closely and do exactly as I say…"

## 68

"Zuza Milasa Salins," Leo repeated, saying the name as though it had some special meaning. "So what happened to her?"

"Already ahead of you," Allissa said, waiting for the search engine results to populate on the hotel's slow Wi-Fi. The results finally filled the screen. Allissa's jaw dropped.

"What? What?" Leo scooted across the bed towards her. He read the headline, too.

*Murder victim named as 28-year-old Zuza Salins.*

"No way," Leo muttered. Allissa clicked the link, and a historical newspaper report filled the screen.

"Zuza Salins was found beaten to death at her home in Riga on the tenth of March, 1993. Her husband is facing charges for murder," Allissa read aloud.

"Let's see if that's the real story," Leo said, pointing at the flash drive. "And let's find out what happened to the husband."

Allissa switched over to the files and ran a check for the week after Emilija — or Zuza — had been killed. She checked the first paragraph of several documents, looking for Zuza's name. On the third one she found it. She laboriously typed the hand-written document into an online translator.

"This is largely the same story," Allissa said, disappointed. "I half expected it to be another cover up. Her body was found, and the husband arrested. He was a well-known drunk, apparently."

"Poor woman," Leo said, exhaling. He stared at the discoloured wall. "I totally just thought, you know... we'd find her."

Allissa nodded. "It had to happen at some point. We can't always find the people we're looking for. People do sometimes just disappear and not come back. Especially when there's stuff like this going on." Allissa pointed at the flash drive.

"Yeah, I know." Leo exhaled, shaking his head. "Let's just hope we can get Andreja back home safely. At least now she'll get to keep her house."

"Yeah, we found out what we needed to. We're up against some powerful forces here. I suppose I owe you fifty quid —"

"Wait a minute," Leo interrupted, sitting upright. "Can you find out where she'd buried?"

"I already have. Rainis Cemetery, here in Riga."

"Okay, good. What do we know about this guy who's taken Andreja?"

"He's an arsehole."

"Granted, but what else?"

"He's pretty powerful and wants access to these files. I bet there're a load of secrets about him buried in here."

"Exactly. Jansons said Mikhail was running for president in a few weeks. He'll be desperate to keep these files under wraps, and by now —"

"He'll probably have figured out we've got them," Allissa cut in.

"That means we're one step ahead." Leo grinned and looked from Jansons' bag on the floor to Allissa beside him. "I think it's time to turn the tables on this thing."

## 69

One of Riga's antique blue and white trams rattled across an intersection. A bell dinged angrily at the waiting traffic shuffling from its path. Then it picked up speed, the cables suspended above pinging with the motion. No sooner had the tram reached speed, then it slowed again. It squealed to a stop and inside, an electronic voice advertised the location.

"This is us," Allissa said, springing to her feet. Leo leapt up too, and they forced their way into a scrum of women already waiting at the doors. Allissa had watched them pass many stops already and noticed that if the passengers weren't quick, the tram would carry on, regardless.

Leo and Allissa fought their way through the doors and stepped out into the late afternoon sunshine. A moment after their feet were on the pavement, the doors snapped shut and the tram accelerated away at a speed that belied its age.

Three hours had passed since Leo and Allissa had formulated their plan. First, Allissa had suggested they both got some rest. They'd been up all night already and if things went as they expected, the night ahead looked to be sleepless, too. Leo had agreed, but even before he tried to close his eyes, he knew that sleep wouldn't come. He stared at the cracked ceiling of the hotel room, listening to the scraping sound of a vacuum running over a threadbare carpet somewhere upstairs. As he'd expected, Allissa slept soundly beside him.

There were a few things to organise and supplies to acquire before they made their way to the cemetery. They'd done this quickly, always looking over their shoulders for would-be pursuers. They'd boarded the tram, heading in the direction of Mežaparks.

Allissa slipped through the heavy steel gate of Rainis Cemetery. They'd carefully researched and noted down both the location of the cemetery and the grave they sought within it. They didn't have time to waste.

Leo stepped alongside Allissa, and they both gazed out at the sprawling cemetery. Leo exhaled slowly through parted lips. The cemetery was like no other he'd seen before. Dense woodland covered the entire area, with the graves set out in orderly rows beneath the thick shade. Leo tightened the straps of Jansons' backpack. The supplies they picked up were heavy.

"This way, I think," Allissa said, leading them down a path lined on both sides by tall silver birches.

Leo glanced first one way, and then the other. It wasn't just the presence of the dense trees that made this cemetery different from the ones he'd seen before. Many of the headstones were different, too. Some were statues, of who Leo assumed must be the deceased. Others were crosses with three horizontal parts, rather than one.

"That's the great thing about going to new places, isn't it?" Allissa said, glancing at Leo.

"What's that?"

"All the differences you notice when you look at something for the first time."

"Yes." Leo examined a headstone shaped out of metal. He glanced at Allissa. "You're totally right."

A man and two children stood around a grave on the left. The largest of the two children removed a bunch of wilted flowers and replaced them with fresh ones. Leo glanced at the flowers in Allissa's hands and wondered about the last time anyone had placed flowers on Emilija's grave. The thought unsettled him. There was something deeply sombre about this case. The poor woman had seen her father killed, been taken from her mother, exposed to who knows what and then finally killed by her drunk husband. It constantly troubled Leo that for all the good he and Allissa did, there would always be people that they couldn't help.

They reached the end of the path. Allissa paused, then looked left and right. To the right sat a small church, its redbrick walls radiating in the bright sunlight.

"This way," Allissa said, leading them to the left.

This section of the cemetery seemed darker and more overgrown. The earth had been cleared of fallen leaves, but the canopy of the trees was thick, casting the whole area in a perpetual gloom. A thick hedge obscured it from the rest of the cemetery. Leo looked upwards. The tall but thin trunks of the birches swayed and swished in a sudden gust of wind.

The area was devoid of colour. As Leo had feared, no flowers had been left here. The headstones were different here too, much more simple than those at the front of the cemetery. A slab of mottled grey stone displayed the name of the deceased, scarred by the ravages of nature and time. Moss and lichen crept in abundance across the stone.

"Zuza Milasa Salins," Allissa muttered, her eyes flicking between the stones as they passed. Reading the decaying words in the low light was a challenge. Leaves rustled nearby. Leo looked up. His breath caught in his throat. Maybe this was it. An eddy of dust spun through the undergrowth and then died to nothing. Somewhere beyond the scrub, a tram clanged and rumbled its way back towards the city.

"I've found her," Allissa said, her voice softer than usual.

Leo turned. Allissa's expression was forlorn, as her eyes fixed on a lichen-covered headstone. Leo stood beside her and slid his arm around her waist. He was sure Allissa shared his sadness.

"That's it," Allissa said, pointing at the headstone.

*Zuza Milasa Salins* was just visible above the date of her death.

"They didn't even have anything to say about her," Allissa said. "No one could even come up with a sentence for her headstone." Allissa cuffed her eyes.

"We can't save everyone," Leo said, pulling her closer. But in his heart, he knew they had to try.

At that moment, the sound of feet thundering across the compacted earth filled the air. Leo and Allissa locked eyes, knowing exactly what was about to happen.

"Stop where you are," a voice shouted.

Allissa pushed something deep within the bunch of flowers and then laid them carefully on the grave.

Three men, all dressed in black, appeared from the undergrowth. Three guns extended towards Leo and Allissa.

Allissa glanced at her newly-purchased watch. "One hour and fifteen minutes left," she whispered to Leo.

Leo nodded almost imperceptibly and looked from one man to the next. He raised his hands slowly.

"Do not move. If you try to run, you will be shot," the familiar voice came again.

This bit, Leo suspected, was going to hurt.

## 70

"Don't think we will not do it." The man's English was impeccable, although accented.

Allissa scanned the assembled men, each of their expressions set in a snarl.

"Your bodies will be dragged from the Daugava in a few months' time by some fisherman."

The man in the centre lowered his weapon and grinned menacingly at Leo and Allissa. He was slighter than the others, with thick brown hair. He moved with like a big cat, muscles rippling beneath his black clothes.

"Your skin will have started to flake away. They'll have to identify you by your teeth. That is, unless we pull them out before letting you go." He stepped out across one of the graves. His black boots stomped across the sacred earth of someone's final resting place. The man's grin broadened.

Allissa's eyes contracted on him. She watched his every move.

"Of course, you've given us some fun in the last few days. First, your escape from the apartment in Zolitūde. Then climbing out of the roof of the cabin. You're very resourceful.

But, I'm afraid we have to bring the fun to an end. We can't have you running all over the city forever. There's an election coming up. Appearances must be maintained." The man's grin widened.

Allissa realised all at once that the man looked like a younger version of Mikhail. "Your dad?" she asked.

The man fixed his gaze on Allissa. His eyes were close together, like the barrels of a shotgun. "Very observant. Ten points. Vilis Mikhail, at your service." Vilis laughed dryly. "My family is going down in the history of this country." His expression turned to steel. "Search them, then cuff them. We have to go."

Leo glanced at the two other men. They were tall, wide hunks of muscle. They looked as though they'd been cut from the same cliff or felled from the same forest. The only discernible difference was that one had bright blonde hair, and the other was bald. They lowered and then holstered their weapons. They stepped across the graves towards Leo and Allissa.

Vilis raised his gun and levelled it at the space between Leo and Allissa.

Blonde Hair trampled across the flowers Allissa had placed on the grave. Allissa glanced at the petals now crushed into the soil.

Baldy stepped up to Leo and snatched Jansons' bag. Leo struggled to remove the straps from his shoulders as the man yanked the bag away.

Allissa took a small step backwards to keep Leo in her peripheral vision. Blonde Hair approached Allissa and began to search her. His thick hands padded from her left wrist to her left shoulder in a practiced motion. His focus moved to Allissa's shoulders.

Baldy tore the backpack open and peered inside.

Allissa tried to swallow, her mouth dry. Leo paled.

Baldy reached into the bag and pulled out a bottle of Black Balsam in a presentation box.

"Pass it here." Vilis lowered the gun and snapped his fingers. Baldy threw the bottle and Vilis caught it adeptly with one hand.

Allissa and Leo exchanged nervous glances. There were three identical boxes in the backpack. The top two contained the Black Balsam, as they should. The one at the bottom contained a little present from Jansons. The plan hinged on the hope that the men wouldn't have time to search all three boxes.

Blonde Hair searched Allissa's right arm.

Vilis snapped open the lid of the presentation box and slid out the bottle of liquor. "Shopping?" he asked, an eyebrow raised.

"Souvenirs, for the family," Leo croaked.

Allissa willed Leo to stay calm. She longed to reach out and take his hand.

Vilis laughed. "You are so predictable." He threw the bottle to the floor. It cracked over Emilija's headstone. Shards of glass peppered the earth, and the liquid ran down across her name.

Blonde Hair finished with Allissa's right arm and now stood directly in front of her. He placed his hands on her sides, then slid them up and across her back.

Baldy dug around in the bag and pulled out the second box of Black Balsam. Allissa's stomach made a fist.

Blonde Hair's hands searched around her stomach and over her breasts. The unwelcome hands, however, were not her main concern right now.

Baldy tore open the box, slid the bottle out, and threw it at the headstone. Liquid exploded across the stone, and glass covered the grave. Baldy dropped the empty box to the floor and shoved his hand back inside the bag.

Allissa watched his muscles tense as he grabbed the last box.

Blonde Hair dropped into a crouch. His hands ran across Allissa's hips and around onto her arse.

Allissa took a deep breath and glanced from one man to the other. One man with his hand in the bag, the other with his hands on her body. She needed to stop this now.

"What are you doing?! Get your hands off me, you creep!" Allissa launched her right knee up and forwards. It connected firmly with Blonde Hair's nose. The nose crunched with breaking bones. "He's trying to touch me up. Get off me." She shoved the man backwards.

Blonde Hair stumbled backwards and sprawled across the grave. His hands shot to his face. He yelped and snarled. Blood streamed down his chin and across the front of his shirt.

Baldy dropped the bottle and the backpack. He fumbled for his gun. The bag crashed to the floor.

A click issued from Vilis's gun. He pointed it directly at Allissa. His hands were steady. "Cuff them and get out of here," he snarled.

Baldy pulled his gun from his holster and raised it at Leo.

Vilis turned his narrow gaze on Allissa. "You'll pay for that."

Allissa smiled sweetly. Blonde Hair grumbled, rising to his feet. He held the bridge of his nose with one hand, then forced Allissa's hands behind her back. He pulled plastic lock ties from his pocket and yanked them tight around Allissa's wrists.

Baldy did the same to Leo.

"Bring the bag," Vilis barked. "We'll need to finish searching it back at the factory." Vilis led the way back through the cemetery.

Allissa glanced back at Emilija's grave, now covered with broken glass and crumped flowers. She made a silent promise that as soon as she was able, she would come back and clear the mess up.

As Blonde Hair shoved her along, Allissa saw something on the headstone. Something she hadn't seen before. Something the alcohol had cleared away.

"Leo," she hissed. "Look at that, the headstone, the date."

Leo glanced around. His eyes narrowed, and the beginnings of an idea formed in his mind.

Maybe things weren't quite as they'd seemed.

## 71

Leo peered through the window of the Mercedes G Class as it coursed back through the streets of Riga. He writhed and wriggled for the first few minutes of the journey, trying to find comfort with his hands still tied behind his back. The bald-headed thug sat between Leo and Allissa, scowling and jabbing his elbows at each of them when they moved. The blonde-haired thug sat in the passenger seat, a roll of blood-soaked tissue held to his nose. He moaned constantly and cast snide glances over his shoulder at Leo and Allissa, leaving Leo under no illusion that he would very much like to hurt them.

Leo pulled a deep breath of the 4x4's warm and stuffy air. The smell of sweat seeped from the man beside him. The stench clawed the back of his throat. He wiggled again and got another elbow to the ribs.

The coil of barbed wire, which had loosened during the day, tightened about Leo's chest again. His anxiety grew.

He attempted to distract himself by watching the clock on the dashboard. He calculated they now had less than an hour to make their play. It had to work.

Suddenly Leo felt well out of his depth. He was drowning, the dirty water slipping over his nose and mouth.

He drew a deep breath, counted to five and turned towards the window. Right now, he needed to stay calm. Things would work out.

The sky was darkening. The various proud architectural styles of the city bathed beneath bright lights. Vilis dropped down a gear and hammered the G Class around a slowing bus. They zipped past the central station, beyond which the curved arches of the former zeppelin hangars that housed the market skulked in the gloom.

The 4x4 followed the railway lines for a few minutes. They slid to a stop at a red traffic signal. Vilis cursed as the lights changed. Leo supposed that Vilis wasn't used to doing what he was told. Maybe in normal circumstances, he would just drive through them. But now, Leo assumed, Vilis wouldn't want to get pulled over by the police. Sure, his father's influence could wash away any charges, but the questions would be inconvenient.

The light above the roadway changed to green. Vilis accelerated hard, forcing Leo back into the seat.

Vilis slung the wheel, and the G Class squealed into a side street. They bumped along between the monolithic walls of dark factories. The crisp, bright lights of the Mercedes bobbed up and down against the decrepit structures.

Leo glanced up at them, silhouettes against the orange glow of the city. Smokeless chimneys clawed at the sky.

Leo concentrated on remembering the details in an attempt to keep his anxiety at bay. He tried to picture each turn they'd made on the journey so far. With the distraction, the barbed wire around his chest loosened. Breath slid into his lungs more easily.

Vilis slowed the G Class to a crawl and then stopped beside a large metal shutter in the factory's wall. Vilis sounded the horn three times.

Leo listened to the engine idling and the heavy breathing of the three men. From the front seat, Blondie grunted through his busted nose.

Metal scraped against metal. Leo glanced around for the source of the screeching. The metal shutter beside them laboured upwards on rusting tracks. Bright light streamed from the factory's interior. As soon as the shutter was high enough, Vilis revved the engine and the G Class slipped inside.

Leo blinked against the harsh light of the factory interior. Colours danced across his vision. Vilis pulled the Mercedes to a stop and killed the engine. The metal shutter ground back down behind them.

The front doors of the 4x4 opened. Vilis and Blondie climbed out and opened the vehicle's rear doors. They pulled Leo and Allissa to their feet.

The room spun around Leo for a few moments. His hands and fingers were numb. He glanced around, again trying to dispel his anxiety by concentrating on something. They were in a warehouse. Steel girders ran from the floor to the ceiling. One wall was made up of obscured, grime-covered windows. The other walls were brick, stained and discoloured. Bright industrial lights washed the centre of the room in a pearlescent glow, but left both ends in shadow. The place appeared to be empty.

The shutter behind them thumped to the floor. Silence fell. Leo glanced at Allissa. She stepped forwards, her hands still tied behind her back, her eyes fixed on something at the far end of the room. Leo spun around to follow her gaze. A door in the far wall swung open, and a figure stepped through.

Leo's jaw hung loose. A ball of iron formed in his throat. His mind roamed for solutions to explain what he was seeing.

The figure stepped further into the light.

"Andreja," Leo muttered. "What the hell?!"

## 72

Andreja stepped into the room. The overhead lights cast a strong beam across her face. Her eyes and neck were left in shadow.

Leo's eyes narrowed. His mind spun through all their conversations, looking for a clue as to how he'd got this so wrong.

"It's so nice to finally meet you," a voice boomed from Andreja's direction. But it was not Andreja's voice.

Leo examined Andreja's expression. Her face was motionless, pensive almost. Leo noticed her posture. Like his, her hands were tied behind her back.

"I hear you've given my son a bit of a run-around."

Leo searched the darkness. Something moved from the door behind Andreja.

"It serves him right. I've always said he's had it too easy. It's about time he had a bit of challenge in his life. But, alas, these games must come to an end." A figure stepped through the door and stood beside Andreja.

"Mikhail," Allissa muttered.

Mikhail embodied the very image of a statesman. His grey hair was carefully styled. His expensive suit impeccably tailored to his slim figure. He was not a tall man, but he exuded a natural confidence and larger-than-life charisma. He smiled and his impossibly white teeth shone. He shared the same dark, close-together eyes as his son. He looked from Leo to Allissa and back again, as though sharing a joke.

"Yes, indeed," Mikhail said, pushing one hand into the pocket of his trousers. The other drew tiny circles in the air. "As I say, it's lovely to finally meet you. Miss Panasenko has told me so much about you."

Leo and Allissa glanced at Andreja. She shook her head almost imperceptibly.

"What do you want from us?" Allissa said, sneering.

"Oh, we'll get to that, don't worry," Mikhail crowed. His voice had a natural resonance that Leo suspected was honed on people listening to his every word.

Vilis stepped forward and spoke to his father in Latvian. Leo looked from father to son. The similarities were striking.

Mikhail examined his son closely. His eyes narrowed and his brow darkened. His response came out in short, sharp bursts. Leo had no idea about the subject of their conversation, but it sounded as though the father wasn't happy with his son.

"I'm sorry." Mikhail turned back towards Leo and Allissa. "How rude of me, you haven't even been offered a seat."

He spat some more words towards Vilis, who shuffled away across the warehouse.

"His mother, God rest her, used to think I was too hard

on him," Mikhail said, his eyes locked on Vilis retreating into the shadows. "But she was wrong. She was too soft on him." Mikhail turned to Leo. "Tell me, what does a man learn if things are easy?"

"Urm, I'm not —"

"Nothing." Mikhail clapped his hands together. The sound boomed through the warehouse. "Nothing is to be learned through ease. That is why this guy" — he pointed into the shadows at the far end of the warehouse where Vilis was clattering about — "took two days to find and capture you. But you see, it is not his fault. People his age are the same all over our country. These young people — like my dear son — have never had the challenge, they've never had to strive, or to do without, or to work hard. They have had milk without looking after the cow. And I am sorry to tell you that it has made them weak. And a weak country is no good to anyone. When I was growing up, it was hard, yes, but with that came glory. And that is the glory I want to restore to this great country." Mikhail spoke the words as though in a rapture.

Vilis appeared from the shadows, carrying a pair of metal chairs. He put them down in the centre of the warehouse and returned to fetch one more.

Mikhail barked some words in Latvia. Blonde Hair and Baldy appeared from behind the car. They pushed Leo and Allissa towards the chairs and forced them to sit. Leo's hands hung awkwardly over the backrest.

Vilis returned with one more chair and forced Andreja to sit. Leo caught her gaze. He had expected her to seem scared and dejected. Fury simmered in her eyes.

"But," Mikhail continued, "not everyone sees it that way. There are some people who would like to see our country continue to stumble along, living off the scraps thrown by other European states. You know, we have spent most of the last century occupied by another power, but people don't think that is enough. They want to hand power over again. We need to be strong —"

"Thanks for the history lesson," Allissa interrupted. "But get to the point."

Mikhail looked at her. His thin lips twisted into a snarl. Then he clasped his hands together and beamed his greatest smile yet. He slapped his thigh with his right hand and roared with laughter. "You have demonstrated my point so excellently." He laughed again. "That is exactly the sort of attitude I want from my team. But, it seems they do not have your... shall I say... spirit."

"Get. To. The. Point," Allissa said, sounding out each word like a petulant teenager.

"Of course, of course. Time is precious. Okay, well. Many years ago, I had some dealings with Miss Panasenko's mother —"

"You betrayed her," Andreja said, speaking for the first time. Her voice was full of bitterness.

Mikhail leaned back on his heels and looked down at Andreja, then glanced at his fingernails. "Such an ugly way to phrase it."

"You betrayed my mother and killed my father," Andreja spat.

Leo and Allissa watched the exchange as if it were a tennis match, heads turning from side to side.

"Yes, I am sorry to say that last part is true. But that was a long time ago. Anyway, when Miss Panasenko's mother escaped to England, she took with her information about the location of a secret file store. This was top secret. Above even my pay grade at the time. I assume that one of her contacts discovered it while they were ferreting around in the woods. Helping criminals escape, or something like that. Knowledge of this was of the highest level, you realise. If I didn't know where it was... well, it just shows you. Anyway, we had orders to track down these people and to... kill is such an ugly word, don't you think?" Mikhail drew another circle with the index finger of his right hand. "Anyway, we had to stop them telling everyone where this file store was. But, alas, Miss Panasenko's mother got out before we could... tie up that loose end. So, when I got a report that Miss Panasenko was back in the country a week ago, with my election coming up, I assumed that she was here to cause trouble."

"You are a murderer! The country deserves to know who they are electing," Andreja snarled.

Mikhail laughed again. He made a fist and held it up in front of his face. "Such passion! Yes! This is what the country needs. This drive. This passion! Maybe you could go into politics too. I'll be looking for ministers this time next month —"

"Never. People will find out what you did. They will see you for who you really are."

Mikhail shook his head slowly. He suddenly became solemn. "No, you see, that is where you're wrong. I accept that the world has changed, that people may find the things I did back then slightly... unpalatable. But that's not a fair judgment. You cannot judge old actions by modern standards —"

"That makes a lot of sense," Leo interrupted, trying to force confidence into his voice.

Mikhail smiled in his direction. "I'm glad you think so, yes."

"It's a great story, and it's the first time I've heard it. I bet you have loads more stories like that. Can we hear another?" Leo said.

Allissa glanced at Leo and then giggled.

Mikhail's gaze narrowed, and then he roared with laughter. "You are so funny. Very funny indeed. We followed you to the file store and watched you escape through the roof. That was very funny too, by the way. Running like rats!" Mikhail's laugher drained, and then he became solemn again. "The body of your friend is still there." Mikhail looked at the fingers on his right hand. "Such a shame he had to die that way. I would hate for the same to happen to the three of you. All I want is what you took; access to the files."

Mikhail shouted another few Latvian words. Blonde Hair appeared, pushing a large metal table on wheels. On top of the table sat the old computer monitor Leo and Allissa had last seen in the cabin. Baldy appeared, carrying the computer's processing unit. He placed it down carefully on the floor beside the table and plugged in the cables.

Blonde Hair glared at Leo and Allissa angrily, and returned to the side of the room to fetch a long power cable. He plugged the computer in and powered it up. The machine hummed and beeped. Blocks of colour flickered on the monitor.

"It pains me to say it, but this is one thing your generation seems to be better at." Mikhail pointed in the direction of the computer. "I have had an expert examine this, but they say it's been corrupted. Whatever you did to this computer while you were in the cabin, you need to undo it now."

Vilis shouted some instructions in Latvian. His voice echoed several times around the enclosed space. Vilis, Blonde Hair and Baldy stepped out from the shadows. Each held a gun. Vilis took aim at Andreja, Baldy levelled his gun at Leo and Blonde Hair — a grin now painted on his bloodied face — pointed his gun at Allissa.

"You will undo it now and get me those files. Or you will die."

## 73

"Yeah, sure, I can sort that for you," Allissa said, looking at the computer's flashing screen.

Leo shot her an anxious glance.

"Very good." Mikhail smiled and rubbed his hands together.

"But I can't do it with my hands tied like this," Allissa said, glancing down at her tethered wrists.

"Of course, of course," Mikhail agreed, striding over to Allissa. He pulled a switchblade from his jacket pocket. He bent down behind Allissa.

The blade's steel was cold against her wrists.

"Just remember," Mikhail said, pushing the side of the blade against her skin. "My men have their guns pointed at you and your friends. Although no one needs to die today, it doesn't mean they won't."

Allissa looked up at Blonde Hair. His nose, still bracketed with blood, was bent and bruised. He stared back at her malevolently. He pushed back his shoulders like a boxer preparing for a fight. His muscles bulged and his neck clicked.

"You have already made a great impression," Mikhail said, sliding the knife beneath the tie that secured Allissa's wrists. The tie snapped.

Allissa's wrists were suddenly free. She rubbed her hands together.

Allissa stood, flexed her shoulders and rubbed her wrists. She glanced down at the watch on her left wrist.

"Three minutes," she said, glancing at Leo for just long enough to see a tiny nod in reply.

"What?" Mikhail said, walking away, no doubt to give his men a clear line of fire should they need it.

"That's how long I reckon this will take me," Allissa said. She pulled the chair up to the computer and sat down again. The computer was mounted on a heavy metal table. Allissa tapped the surface. It clanged, deep and metallic.

Blonde Hair groaned in frustration, his weapon levelled directly at Allissa. Allissa looked up at him and smiled. His mouth twisted into a sneer. The weapon held firm.

Mikhail spoke in Latvian, and Blonde Hair swore again. Allissa knew he would take great pleasure in killing her. She had to make sure he didn't get the chance.

Allissa examined the computer. It was reporting a fault with one of the hard drives. That was because Allissa had corrupted all the data back in the cabin. It was irreversible, but the men surrounding them obviously didn't know that. She tapped a few keys and went into the settings menu. For now, she needed to make it appear as if she was playing ball. She glanced down at her watch.

She peered over her shoulder at Leo. He was several feet to her left, so would be further away from the explosion. Hopefully far enough away not to be too disorientated. He too would be counting down the seconds.

Allissa glanced over at the Mercedes G Class, about a

dozen feet to her right. The doors remained open. She saw the backpack in the foot well of the rear seats. Hopefully it would deliver enough of a punch from there.

She tapped into another menu and scrolled through the settings. "Ah, I think I've almost got it now." She made a change to a few of the boot settings. It wouldn't make any difference; the data was in pieces.

Allissa looked down at the watch again.

The sound of her pulse rumbled in her ears, marking the passing of time. If her calculations were correct, they had less than a minute. The beat of her heart picked up pace.

Allissa cleared her throat and rubbed her wrists. Fortunately, the numbness had almost faded.

"What's happening?" Mikhail said.

"I've got to change the start up sequence," Allissa said. "It's booting in the wrong order. Come here and I'll show you." She beckoned him over.

Mikhail's dark eyes contracted. "Just do it," he snarled.

Blonde Hair grumbled. The gun shook in his thick hands.

Allissa met Mikhail's stare. She once again got the impression that she was looking down the barrels of a shotgun. There was something inhuman about him.

She tried to swallow, but her throat was dry. Her heart thundered now. She broke the stare and glanced quickly down at her watch. "I think we should be there in a few seconds now," she said, trying to make her voice sound calm. "I need to manually restart it."

Allissa leaned down to access the machine beneath the desk. Several LEDs blinked furiously from the discoloured plastic. She looked again at her watch. Five seconds.

She peered behind and caught Leo's eye. "Four... three..." she mouthed silently.

Leo planted his feet solidly on the floor. The muscles in his neck and arms stood rigid, ready for action.

"Two..." Allissa whispered. She raised her voice. "Hold on, it's..." — she crawled further beneath the desk — "I've almost got it, wait — "

A screeching, whooshing and crunching noise vibrated through the warehouse. A bright white light filled the room. It strobed several times and died.

A deafening boom followed. It roared, howled, and bellowed.

Allissa clamped her hands over her ears. She cowered beneath the table.

She hoped that Leo and Andreja were far enough away. The noise and light swirled above her like a maelstrom of destruction.

A wave of heat passed over her, searing skin and air. Broken glass scattered. The deep thunder of hungry flames roared. Allissa hadn't expected there to be flames, as there weren't any last time. She glanced over at the Mercedes. Smoke billowed from the windows, and the first orange tendrils of fire tickled through the front grill.

Last time the thing had exploded in a room. Not in a vehicle.

Allissa took a deep breath and erupted with energy. She sprung upwards and flipped the table over. The heavy computer monitor crashed to the floor. Broken glass and twisted shards of plastic skittered across the concrete. Electricity sparked from the damaged power line.

Allissa dared a look over her shoulder at Leo. He was lying on his side. Panic welled within her for a moment — was he okay?

He pushed himself across the floor using his feet. His arms were still fastened behind his back. Allissa grabbed one leg of the table and dragged it towards Leo. It scraped noisily across the floor. After a few feet, the weight became too much. Allissa darted across to Leo and dragged him behind the table.

"Thanks," Leo said, panting. He slid up with his back against the table. His words tumbled out. There wasn't time. "What's happening over there? We need to get Andreja and get out of here."

Allissa peered over the edge of the heavy table. She expected to see the men climbing dozily to their feet, scrabbling around for their guns and preparing for the final attack. What she saw was something quite different.

"What the hell?" Allissa gasped, taking in, but not quite understanding the scene before her.

## 74

Andreja's instinct kicked in as the explosion roared. She threw herself to the floor, her body crashing hard into the concrete. Her bones shook and pain surged. She kept her head as low as possible as the cacophony of breaking glass and thumping flames rattled and raged behind her.

She listened to her body. Her heart beat more quickly now. Like it had all those years ago, when fighting was a way of life. Every moment counted. Every firing synapse was a step in the right direction. A small victory. An inch towards freedom.

The sounds of the explosion died away. The ringing continued to sound in Andreja's ears. That was natural. She didn't have time to wait for that to subside. There would be time to recover later. Now it was all about action.

Andreja rolled over onto her elbow. Ribbons of glass crunched beneath her movement. She inspected the scene before her. Smoke rose from the 4x4, its windows blown out and its paintwork charred.

She was lucky enough to have been the farthest one

away from the blast, and though her ears were ringing, her vision was fine. The instinct to flatten herself against the concrete had helped.

Her eyes locked on Mikhail and his men. Vilis was scrambling to his feet, his eyes roaming unfocused around the warehouse. The others were still sprawled out on the floor.

Again, a beat of instinct pulsed through Andreja's body. She tucked her knees up against her stomach and rolled on to her feet. With tremendous effort, she stood. She was shaky at first, but balance soon returned.

Vilis, still climbing unsteadily to his feet, shouted at his men. Blonde Hair moaned and slithered impotently across the floor. His gun lay on the floor a few feet away. Baldy groaned, but hadn't yet started moving. Mikhail appeared to be out cold.

Andreja read the scene and then focused. Intuition took over. Her heart boomed. The pulse of revenge flowed through her veins. Every sense and synapse was primed, waiting for her instruction. She assessed the threats. Her training kicked in and she ordered them by threat level. With another glance between the four men, she ran.

Andreja ran for Vilis. She closed the distance in three paces. Her hands were still tied. He would have the advantage of strength. But speed and surprise were hers. Andreja intended to use them. She landed on her left foot and swung straight into a right kick. She threw her whole body into the motion. This kick could save her life.

Vilis glanced up at the incoming kick at the last moment. His eyes constricted. He looked up at Andreja. Her shin connected with his neck. The crack jarred through her leg, almost knocking her off balance. Vilis fell to the floor.

His head bounced on the concrete; his arms splayed out behind him.

She landed the kick perfectly and spun, twisting her upper body to maintain balance. Her heart was beating in tune now. Her eyes scanned the surrounding scene again.

Vilis lay on the floor, unmoving. Dead or unconscious, he wasn't Andreja's immediate concern. Her gaze locked on Blonde Hair, who struggled towards his gun.

Andreja closed the distance quickly. She reached the man as his thick hand closed across the metal. She landed a heel over his knuckles. She pushed her entire weight down on the back of the man's hand and twisted. Bones crunched and Blonde Hair wailed. Andreja didn't waste a single moment. She kicked the gun away. It was useless to Andreja without the use of her hands.

She dug the toes of her right foot beneath his chest and rolled him over. Surprised by the movement, and still reeling from the pain in his hand, Blonde Hair offered no resistance. He splayed across the concrete.

Andreja took a step back and swung a solid kick towards his unprotected skull. Blonde Hair's head jarred forwards. He fell still.

Andreja paused, breathing heavily. She looked around the warehouse.

Thick black smoke poured from the 4x4. Flames flickered from the engine.

She looked back at the men. Baldy was coming to his senses. He crawled shakily towards his gun, which lay on the floor nearby. The man glanced fearfully over his shoulder at Andreja. He lay a few feet away from the firearm.

Andreja ran at him.

The man's hand closed over the gun. He lifted it from the floor. He rolled, turned, and levelled the gun at Andreja.

Andreja gritted her teeth and leapt. The gun howled. A bullet pounded through the air. It whizzed somewhere past her.

Baldy attempted to aim again, but Andreja was too close. She curled up her feet and came down on the man's chest with her knees. Ribs cracked beneath her. The man yelped in pain. Without even thinking, Andreja twisted and trapped the man's neck beneath her shin. She reached her tethered hands down behind her and pulled her foot upwards, further constricting his neck.

Andreja gazed down. Baldy's eyes bulged from his sockets. First, colour drained from his skin, and then he turned blue. He tried to raise the gun, but Andreja kicked it away with her other foot. Finally, he stopped struggling.

Andreja pulled a deep breath. Adrenaline still pounded through her veins. She hadn't experienced that feeling in a very long time. She climbed shakily to her feet.

"Move another inch and I'll blow your head off," came Mikhail's voice from behind her.

## 75

"Okay, the show's over. Come out from there now."

Leo and Allissa peered out from across the table. Mikhail held Andreja at gun point. Vilis sat up bleary-eyed, rubbing his neck. The two thugs lay quietly. Leo couldn't see whether they were still breathing.

Mikhail shouted at his son in Latvian. The younger man struggled to his feet and picked up one of the guns.

"That was a pretty good show," Mikhail said to Andreja. "You move quickly for a... what is it you do?"

"I teach politics at a university."

Mikhail cracked a smile. "Following in your mother's footsteps, I see. She would be proud. You have some unusual skills for a teacher."

Leo had to admit that Mikhail was right. The speed at which Andreja had moved and disabled three men was nothing short of miraculous. He was beginning to see the quiet and unassuming woman in a new light. Another note of realisation chimed within him. He examined the thought. Right now, it didn't really make sense. He couldn't fit the facts together. He played with the ideas silently for a few seconds before storing them away for later.

Another explosion thumped from the burning car. Flames licked up above the windscreen. One of the door panels melted. Leo watched liquid run across the floor nearby.

"Anymore funny business and I'll put a bullet in each of you," Mikhail said, his eyes darting from Andreja to the table behind which Leo and Allissa still hid. "Get out from there. Now."

Leo looked around, searching for options. He was exposed and useless with his hands tied behind his back.

The 4x4 burned furiously. Flames shimmered across the bonnet. Leo tasted the acrid smell of burning plastic and rubber in the air. He glanced upwards. Thick black smoke swirled across the ceiling and out through a couple of the glassless window frames.

Being this close to a raging fire bought back nasty memories of their recent trip to Hong Kong. It was a case that almost ended in disaster. They needed to get out of here now.

Leo examined the floor nearby for anything that could help. He saw a long shard of twisted metal two feet to his right. One edge looked sharp. Leo leaned backwards and seized it in his hands. He spun it around. The metal cut against his skin. It was sharp. He pushed it between his wrists and out of sight.

"Get up now!" Mikhail shouted. Vilis cocked his gun and took a step towards them.

Allissa climbed to her feet and helped Leo up. Leo glanced down again and noticed the damaged cables of the computer. When the monitor fell from the metal table, the power cable had been torn from the back. This cable now lay with its wires exposed, a few inches from Leo's shoe.

A door panel, disfigured by the heat, clattered to the floor. A flurry of sparks shot across the concrete. Leo glanced again at the growing pool of liquid beneath the car.

"That way," Vilis snarled, signalling that Leo and Allissa should stand near Andreja.

Something else shattered, and the flames intensified.

Leo rubbed the shard of metal against his bindings. It was slow work.

Leo and Allissa took a step in the direction indicated.

Vilis and Mikhail exchanged some tense words. Both glanced at the burning vehicle.

Leo pushed hard against the makeshift knife. Pain surged through his fingers. The serrated edge dug into his bindings.

Vilis glanced behind him again.

"We should probably get out of here," Allissa said nonchalantly. "Shame, it was a nice car." She nodded towards the Mercedes, now consumed with howling flames.

"Shut up," Vilis snarled.

Leo suspected they were running without a plan now. Mikhail wouldn't have predicted being turfed from their hideout by the people they'd kidnapped.

Flames cracked and snapped from the G Class. Liquid pooled across the floor, spreading towards the far wall of the warehouse.

"Surely the fire brigade will be here soon." Leo had to raise his voice over the sound of the flames. His muscles tensed in his efforts to sever the bindings. "The smoke will be visible from miles away."

A tyre popped, the sigh of rushing air lost in the roaring

flames. The 4x4's suspension groaned and clanged as the car dropped onto the wheel's rim.

Leo pushed harder against the metal. It dug. His hands moved more freely. The metal's sharp edge snapped through the final strands of plastic. The metal buried itself in Leo's forearm. He winced, but worked hard to hide it from his expression.

"Shut up," Vilis repeated. "Everything is under control, right father?"

Mikhail nodded.

Leo didn't believe him.

Mikhail and Vilis glanced back at the burning car. Leo took his chance. He ducked forwards, tensed his shoulders and ran at Vilis. Leo collided with the man, knocking the gun skywards. Vilis stumbled backwards. His feet slipped over the glass-strewn concrete. He struggled to regain his balance.

Andreja took her chance, too. Ducking beneath the level of Mikhail's gun, she surged forward, knocking Mikhail off balance.

Mikhail's finger curled around the trigger. A succession of bullets hummed through the air in a useless arc.

Andreja swept out her legs and tripped Mikhail to the floor. He fell heavily to the concrete. Allissa charged across and pulled the gun away from his grip.

Vilis took a step backwards, trying to correct his balance. Then another. Leo charged again and pushed him further. Vilis collapsed across the metal table with a clang. He fell amid the shards of broken plastic and metal that had once been the computer.

Leo ran for the table and snatched up the live cable, which had been torn from the computer monitor as it fell. Leo seized the cable and jabbed the live ends into Vilis's bare neck. For a moment, nothing happened. Then the man shook uncontrollably. His gun crashed to the floor. Leo kicked the gun beneath the burning car. Once the man was disarmed, Leo pulled the cable away.

"We need to get out of here, now!" he shouted. The flames licked across the front of the car now, clawing towards the ceiling. The air hummed with the deep thump of combustion. It wouldn't be long before the heat and smoke made the room inhabitable.

Allissa bent down and pulled the flip-knife from Mikhail's jacket pocket. She cut Andreja's hands free in one stroke. Andreja rubbed the life back into her wrists.

"What about these?" Allissa asked, pointing at Mikhail and Vilis.

Mikhail groaned. Vilis blinked hazily.

Leo scowled. He glanced at the fire. He shook his head. "We'll have to take them with us. Quickly."

Leo grabbed Vilis by the shoulders. The man was heavier than Leo had expected. Leo gritted his teeth and dragged the man towards the metal shutters.

The heat was unbearable now. Flames raged above the roof of the 4x4. The smoke, which had been swirling around the ceiling, now filled the warehouse.

Allissa and Andreja followed Leo, dragging Mikhail by his arms.

Leo thumped a button on the wall, and the large door rattled upwards. As soon as the gap was big enough, they pulled the two men outside.

Fed by the incoming draft, the fire raged more violently. Sound and heat hammered against Leo's back.

He stepped out into the lane and hauled Vilis down the road. When he was a safe distance from the fire, he dropped the man onto the tarmac. Vilis groaned. His eyes fluttered open and then closed again.

Allissa and Andreja followed, dropping Mikhail next to his son.

Leo, Allissa and Andreja ducked back into the building and dragged Blonde Hair and Baldy out too. They dumped the thugs a safe distance from the raging fire.

Leo bent over and took three deep breaths. The noxious smoke weighed heavily on his lungs. Leo coughed and spat.

An explosion rattled through the building behind them. The remaining glass shattered from the warehouse's windows, covering the road outside in diamond shapes shards. Flames leapt out into the night. Black smoke cloaked the building in a dirty shroud. Somewhere nearby an alarm yelped and whined, its sound masked by the howling flames.

Andreja bent down and searched Mikhail's pockets. Her hands moved with practiced efficiency across his jacket and trousers. Mikhail lifted a hand in an attempt to stop her. It fell back to the ground before it even reached her.

Andreja pulled a smartphone from the inside pocket of his jacket. She forced Mikhail's finger onto the pad. The phone unlocked. Andreja dialled a number and held the phone to her ear.

Leo couldn't hear the conversation but watched the woman, silhouetted against the fire, talk into the phone. Allissa stepped beside Leo and also watched her.

Leo considered the ease with which Andreja had taken on the thugs, despite her hands being tied. The idea rose to the top of his mind again. Leo examined it, but still couldn't make sense of it. Something hadn't yet clicked into place.

The distant sounds of sirens now filled the air.

Andreja finished her call, then walked back to the burning door of the warehouse and threw the phone inside.

"We have to go. We're being picked up in fifteen. One kilometre to the east." Andreja pointed. "But there's something I need to do before we go."

## 76

For many years Andreja had fantasised about getting revenge against the man who had killed her father and pulled her family apart. She had pictured it in graphic detail, the pain and misery she longed to cause.

The sound of sirens thumped through the air now. They would be here soon. She must act quickly.

Mikhail lay on the road before her. His suit was blackened, and his skin was smeared from the ravages of fire. Dying in the gutter was a suitable ending for a man like him.

The fire tore its way through the warehouse roof. A support crashed down inside the building, sending a spray of sparks up into the night sky.

Andreja turned away from the noise. She dropped to one knee and clasped her hands around Mikhail's neck. Tendons moved beneath his papery skin. She tightened her grip. A gurgling sound came from his mouth.

Mikhail raised a hand in an attempt to fight her off. It pushed against her forearm, but there was no power there. The arm slumped to the road.

Andreja constricted her grip. Mikhail's breathing weakened. His pulse slowed beneath her fingers. His chest shook and then stopped moving.

Mikhail's eyes fluttered open and closed. They looked colourless in the fire's dancing light.

"Stop," Allissa whispered, placing a hand on Andreja's shoulder. "Stop. It's over."

"No," Andreja hissed, her resolve fortifying. "This man killed my father and tore my family apart. He needs to die."

Mikhail gasped. Spittle flew from his lips.

Another crash resonated from the burning warehouse. A window shattered and a flaming wooden beam thumped to the floor.

"He'll face charges. He won't get away with this." Allissa's grip tightened on Andreja's shoulder.

"No, he won't. He'll make it all go away, like he has for his whole life. There's no justice in court for men like this. No justice. This is the only justice." Andreja tightened her grip again.

Mikhail gurgled and hissed. His hands scraped helplessly at the tarmac.

"No Andreja, we have the files —"

Andreja let go of Mikhail's throat and looked up at Allissa. The light of the flames danced across her face. Her eyes sparkled. "You mean, they weren't on that computer?"

"They were," Allissa said, helping Andreja to her feet. "They were, but now we have the only copy."

Mikhail gurgled as air rushed into his lungs again.

"Where are they? Not in your hotel room? They would have searched there."

"They're somewhere safe," Allissa said, leading Andreja away from Mikhail's stricken body. "They're being looked after. We need to get out of here now. Which way?"

Blue lights strobed through the smoke.

Without looking back, Andreja led Leo and Allissa away, just as a fire engine turned into the street.

## 77

Andreja broke into a slow jog as they rounded the corner.

Leo's legs burned. He was used to a leisurely jog along Brighton seafront, but not running through Riga's industrial landscape after nearly forty-eight straight hours without a rest.

"We don't have much time," Andreja shouted over her shoulder. "The RV point's not far."

Those words struck another chord with Leo. *RV point.* He watched Andreja turning the corner ahead. The phrase seemed incongruous for someone who had blundered into this.

Andreja turned right and led them down a single carriageway road. Leo glanced up at a monolithic factory building, rearing high into the dark night sky. Pipes and wires sprouted from the sheer concrete walls. Beyond the factory, some miles back towards Riga, the light on the top of the Television Tower glowed through the clear sky.

Andreja stopped suddenly, her head turning this way and that. Leo almost ran into the back of her.

"In here," Andreja shouted, pushing them into a recessed doorway. Sirens wailed through the night air. A fire engine followed by two police cars screamed around the corner and howled past in a storm of blue lights and pinging dust. The vehicles slowed and turned at the end of the street towards the burning warehouse.

Colours danced across Leo's vision. Allissa breathed heavily beside him.

"Okay, let's go." Andreja led them back out onto the street at a jog. "We should be there in five minutes."

Andreja led them down two more narrow, dark roads. They weaved past abandoned cars, overflowing bins and stacks of scrap metal.

Eventually they emerged from a gloomy passageway and onto a well-lit road.

"Wait," Andreja hissed, stepping back into the shadows.

Leo peered out at the road. The traffic was light. A pair of heavily-laden lorries chugged past, their bright white lights cutting through the orange glow of the overhead streetlights. Whatever they carried was strapped down tight beneath grey tarpaulins. The diesel growl of their strong engines faded to nothing. Wind whistled through the wires. Metal clanged from one of the factories. Leo wasn't sure why, but he found the whole scene sombre. Decay and deterioration seemed to be the only powers at work here.

Another pair of headlights cut through the gloom. Andreja glanced towards them. A black van materialised. Its engine hummed over the impatient wind.

The van neared and began to slow. There was a logo printed in gold on the van's side, which shone under the glowing streetlights. Leo stared at it. A sense of familiarity twisted deep within him. The van pulled to a stop at the curb before Leo's recognition had bubbled to the surface.

*Ozolin's Wine Merchants*

"This is us," Andreja said, leading them out of the shadow and crossing to the van. She pulled open the passenger door and hopped in.

Leo looked from the logo to Allissa. Surprise was etched across her face, too.

"Ozolin's Wine Merchants," Leo whispered. "That makes perfect sense."

"Are you coming?" Andreja bellowed from the front seat.

## 78

"They figured it out in less than ten minutes," Ozolin said, glancing across at Leo and Allissa. "That's pretty good going to be fair."

Andreja nodded and glanced at Leo and Allissa beside her. They were all squeezed together in the front of the van. For once, Leo didn't mind. It felt good to be safe, warm, and not have anyone following them.

"You've got some explaining to do," Allissa said, glancing at Andreja.

"Yes," Andreja said, meeting Allissa's gaze. "But first I need those files. We'll go and get them now, and then I'll tell you everything."

Allissa held Andreja's gaze for a few seconds. "Okay, but we need to know everything."

Allissa gave their destination. Ozolin raised an eyebrow and pulled away.

They passed very few other cars on their journey back through the city. Groups of people wandered from one bar to the next. The occasional gulp of loud music streamed through an open door.

Theirs was the only vehicle on the road when they pulled up outside Ranis Cemetery. They bundled down from the front seat. Allissa stretched.

Andreja marched up to the cemetery's heavy steel gates. A padlock and chain were draped between them. Andreja looked at it for a moment and then scrambled over the fence with ease. Allissa glanced at Leo. Very little was surprising her about Andreja now.

Leo, Allissa and Ozolin scrambled laboriously across. Ozolin pulled out a torch. The strong beam swept between the densely-packed trees and headstones. Shadows danced in the cracks between light and dark.

Leo and Allissa led them down the central path. The path was lined by the large birch trees, their silver bark shining pearlescent in the beam of Ozolin's torch. They reached the far end of the cemetery and turned left.

A gust of wind hushed and whistled through the trees. Something rustled in the undergrowth.

The cemetery was darker here. The canopy blotted out light from the sky and dense undergrowth covered all sides. Ozolin's torch swept across the headstones.

Allissa and Leo reached the unassuming headstone inscribed with the name *Zuza Milasa Salin*. Shards of glass still sparkled from the surrounding earth. Allissa stepped up to the grave and picked up the discarded flowers. The broken petals, smashed by the heavy boots of the thugs, fell in a shower to the floor.

Allissa turned the flowers over and dug her fingers deep within the stems.

"There you go," she said, holding up the flash drive in the strong beam of the torch. "Now you owe us an explanation."

## 79

Ozolin produced a small laptop from a bag and sat cross-legged on the earth. He inserted the USB. The documents loaded. Ozolin's quick features froze in the glow of the screen. Andreja rushed over and stared at the screen. Ozolin tapped through several documents. Andreja and Ozolin spoke in short bursts of Latvian. When they looked up at Leo and Allissa, they were grinning.

"This is it," Andreja said. "Because of these documents, justice can finally be served for hundreds, if not thousands, of people in this country. Thank you."

"You should have told us about this," Leo said. "We came here to find your sister" — he pointed at Zuza's grave — "and we did. But I suspect you know that already."

Andreja looked at the grave and nodded slowly.

"You knew she was dead before we even left, didn't you?" Allissa said.

Andreja nodded again. She locked eyes with Allissa and then Leo. "I didn't want you to come, remember. This was my mother's idea. I wasn't going to come at all, but then when we found the map, I knew that I had to. This was the last chance to get justice for many people. The last chance before Mikhail became president and made irreversible changes to this country. I contacted Ozolin before I left, and he agreed to help me. We didn't want you to get involved, but knew there was a risk I would be compromised—"

There it was again, Leo thought. *Compromised* wasn't the sort of word he would expect a university lecturer to use. He pulled the semi-formed idea from the depths of his memory, slotted the word in, and examined it again.

"I made sure we wouldn't be seen together in the hope they'd assume I was working alone," Andreja said. "Then, while they interrogated me, you would find the files. I did some research on you; you're very capable investigators and you can move almost unseen around the city because people assume you're tourists. I knew that if anyone could do this, it would be you."

"You used us," Allissa said. "You should have been honest with your intentions."

Andreja nodded. "Perhaps. But the fight is bigger than a single soldier —"

"The fight is bigger than a single —" Leo repeated the phrase, also slotting that into his forming idea. The realisation hit him like a fist to the chest.

"Oh my gosh," Leo said, his eyes springing wide. The barbed wire around his stomach clenched tighter.

Allissa, Andreja and Ozolin looked at Leo.

Leo, silenced by shock, looked from the dates on the grave to Andreja and back again.

"You," he stuttered, barely able to control his words. "That makes perfect sense. Why didn't I see this before…"

## 80

Silence swirled around the cemetery for long seconds.

Allissa's dark eyes flicked from Leo to Andreja and then on to the headstone. She opened her mouth to speak, but no words came forth.

Andreja, crouching beside Ozolin, looked up at Leo.

Leo swallowed. His throat was rough and dry. His breath caught in mid-inhale. He stood tensed on the precipice of success or failure. He was about to make the most ridiculous claim of their investigative careers, or he'd cracked this to the bone.

Andreja's intense stare riveted him to the spot. Leo tried to speak, but words failed him. He took a deep breath, his head shaking slowly. This was the only way the pieces fit together. It just worked. Leo heard the sound of his voice in the silent cemetery.

"You're Emilija."

Andreja stood motionless for long seconds. She turned away from Leo and Allissa's expectant gaze.

Leo's mind spun with things he should say. Nothing

came out. The idea remained fully formed in his mind's eye. He had to be correct.

Andreja's shoulders slumped. She turned back to face them. Tears glistened from her cheeks in the torchlight.

"I've never told anyone this. I thought it would be my secret to take to the grave." Andreja's voice was little more than a whisper. "You're right, I am Emilija."

Allissa's jaw drooped. The panic drifted from Leo's body. The cool night air slipped deep into his lungs.

"When my father was killed, by Mikhail" — she spat the words — "I was taken into care of the state. A new name. A new identity."

"Zuza Milasa Salin," Allissa muttered.

"Yes. Growing up, I was always top of the class. Good, both physically and academically, so I was sent to the University of Latvia, after which I was recruited into the Secret Service. But I didn't want to do it. I was spying for the country that killed my father and ripped my family apart. My guilt grew with every job. All I wanted to do was run, but I couldn't. I was at breaking point when a man came and asked me if I would hand information on to a contact in West Germany. I agreed. That's how I got to know Ozolin."

A shadow slipped from the woman's posture. She stood taller and more confident, as though she were shaking off a mask that had held her back for years. She was Emilija.

Emilija and Ozolin exchanged a glance. A faint smile played on the corners of Ozolin's lips. Leo imagined the nostalgic thoughts spooling through his mind's eye.

"You were a double agent?" Leo said.

"Of sorts, yes. It came naturally to me. It was easy and felt like I was doing the right thing. It was all going well until my husband found out. He was a nasty, drunk man. He said if I ever left him, he would get me taken away. Again, I was trapped."

"So, who is —" Allissa pointed at the headstone.

"In 1993 a miracle happened — I call it a miracle because I can't imagine any other way to describe it. Andreja came from England to attend the university on a year-long exchange programme. As soon as I saw the document with her name on, I knew it was her. When she arrived a few weeks later, it was incredible." Tears rolled freely down Emilija's face now. Thirty years of pain and resentment welled forth.

Leo and Allissa hung on every word.

"We spent many hours together over the next few months. We had years to catch up on." Emilija placed her head in her hands and took a deep breath. "A month before she was due to leave, Andreja came to me with a plan. She wanted me to travel to England with her. To come and live. Leave my husband, leave the world of secrets and lies. But it wasn't that easy. There was no way I would get the permission to travel at that time. We came up with a plan. I was to travel first on Andreja's passport. We both looked very alike, almost identical. I would then send it back for her to follow a few days later. It was all worked out so well. We waited until my husband was out filling himself with drink, as he did every day at my expense, and went to our house to collect my things. We packed the suitcase and were leaving when he came home early. In his drunken stupor, he didn't realise what was happening until he saw the suitcase, then lashed out. Andreja was closest. She fell down the stairs." Emilija's body was wracked with sobs. "I had a decision to make and a few moments to make it. I grabbed Andreja's passport and ran."

Pre-dawn bird song drifted through the cemetery.

"I thought mother would notice, but she was so absorbed in her career. Soon she became ill and was confused anyway." Her voice trailed into silence. "Then she started getting confused anyway, that was the first sign of her illness. Other than that, it was easy. Andreja led a pretty solitary life. Anyone she met regularly didn't know her that well. She went to work, came home, and that was about it."

More tears flowed as Emilija concluded her explanation. "If it weren't for me, she would still be alive. If it weren't for Mikhail, we would all be alive."

Allissa stepped forwards and hugged her. "This is not your fault," she whispered into the woman's ear. Allissa knew how dark secrets tore you up inside. She had travelled halfway around the world, hoping and failing to get away from hers. After a few minutes, Emilija's violent sobbing subsided.

"Let's get this place cleared up," Leo said, looking down at the broken glass. For the next few minutes, they collected the glass shards and placed them in a nearby bin.

Emilija sunk to her knees, her hands touching the earth, below which her long dead sister was finally at peace.

"Let's go," Allissa said, touching Leo on the elbow. "We've done what we came to do."

Leo and Allissa turned and walked to the end of the row of graves. They paused and stared back at Emilija, her face inches from the earth.

"This isn't the way it should end," Leo said, watching Emilija. Allissa's hand closed around his. "All that life, wasted."

"We've done everything we can," Allissa said, leading Leo through the pre-dawn light towards the cemetery's gate. Leo took a deep breath of the crisp morning air. Allissa's fingers tightened around his. Birds skipped between the trees around them, and somewhere a tram rumbled across an intersection. Another morning was coming. Another chance to start over.

"We'll come back with some fresh flowers before we leave," Allissa said, her eyes sweeping over the grand headstones around them. Another chance to start over for some of us, Allissa thought.

Leo agreed, a flurry of emotion welling through him. He turned and pulled Allissa in close.

"I love... I love... urrm, what we do," Leo said, letting the air escape his parted lips.

"Me too," Allissa said, kissing his neck. "So much."

Allissa pulled away and strode towards the gates. "Oh, by the way," she said, turning, her smile radiating in the dusty dawn light. "You owe *me* fifty quid now."

# 81

Marvin Merrowford scrambled out of the Saab and looked out at the diamond surface of the sea far below. He pulled a handkerchief from his jacket and swept it across his forehead. It came away damp. A bright red convertible sports car hummed passed, the grey hair of its driver buffeted by the breeze. Merrowford watched the car pause at the end of the road and turn in the direction of Pett Level. That's the sort of car he should have. He'd worked long and hard enough to afford it, surely.

But summer was on the wane, Merrowford reminded himself. Autumn would be here soon, and people with their convertible cars would be no better off than anyone else.

Merrowford grabbed his briefcase from the backseat and sauntered towards the cottage. He pushed open the iron gate. It creaked on rusting hinges. Insects buzzed around the honeysuckle, which arched its way over the path. Merrowford reached the door and took a deep breath of the heavily-perfumed air. He hadn't seen Andreja since the day he'd revealed the terms of her mother's inheritance. Merrowford hoped that, working with the detectives, she had come up with something to satisfy those terms. He hated being the one to enforce painful rulings. Merrowford cleared his throat and knocked three times on the thick wooden door.

"Miss Panasenko," Merrowford said as the door swung open. "It's so good to see you. I trust you're —"

"Hi," Allissa said brightly, looking up at the red-faced solicitor.

"Miss Stockwell, uh, it's great to see you too."

"Allissa, please," Allissa said, showing the solicitor into the kitchen, where Emilija and Leo sat at the table.

"Thank you for coming," Emilija said. "Please sit down. We have some news."

Merrowford took the chair opposite Emilija and placed his suitcase on the floor. He glanced from Emilija to Leo and then at a folder that lay in the centre of the table. Allissa took a seat at the head of the table.

Emilija picked up the folder, flipped open the lid and tipped out the contents. Several printed documents slid onto the table-top. She passed one to Merrowford.

Merrowford accepted the document. Without his glasses, the text danced in front of his eyes. He pulled his glasses from his inside pocket of his jacket and slid them on. The text steadied and focused before his eyes. It was a copy of an identity document.

"Zuza Milasa Salin," he slowly read. Much of the other writing he couldn't make sense of. "Who is she?"

"This is the name they gave Emilija," Allissa said. "When they put her in the care of the state, they changed her name."

Merrowford nodded and glanced at the others around the table.

Emilija dug another sheet of paper from the folder and slid it across the table. Merrowford turned it over. It was a copy of a black-and-white photograph of a woman in her thirties. Merrowford squinted at the photograph, trying to work out why it seemed strangely familiar. He glanced up at Emilija.

"Strange," — Merrowford paused and looked at the woman sat opposite him — "she looks like you. I suppose she is your sister."

Leo, Allissa and Emilija exchanged glances.

"Where is she now?" Merrowford laid the photograph down carefully on the table.

Emilija dug another document from the folder and presented it to Merrowford. "Zuza Salin's death certificate."

Merrowford nodded sagely as Emilija explained how they'd found the files and tracked down the identity of her sister. When she'd finished, Merrowford reached down, snapped open his briefcase and pulled out a thick wedge of documents.

"Your mother asked that you make efforts to find Emilija. You have gone far above and beyond that. I'll get you to sign these now and I'll start the transfer of assets in the next few days." Merrowford pulled a silver pen from his top pocket. "If you could please sign here, here and here." He spun the documents around.

Emilija accepted the pen and pulled the stack of papers towards her. The pen's nib hovered above the paper.

"There's one more thing you need to know," Emilija said, accepting the pen.

Merrowford raised an eyebrow.

Emilija signed her name and spun the papers back towards Merrowford.

The solicitor read the name, his face contorting in confusion.

"And one more thing," Emilija said, looking up at

Merrowford. No one expected what Emilija said next. "How quickly can I sell this place? I think it's time for me to go home."

Merrowford didn't hear a thing. He read and re-read the name on the document in front of him, his mind trying to make sense of it all.

*Emilija Panasenko.*

## 82

"I didn't see that coming at all, did you?" Leo said, leaving the dual carriageway and heading in the direction of Brighton city centre. The air of the summer evening streamed through the open windows of the Fiat Panda. Even with the warm weather, the car still smelled damp.

"Nope, not at all," Allissa said. "It's great though. She said an opportunity came up to teach politics at the University of Latvia."

"Following in her mother's footsteps."

"Well, let's hope not." Allissa grinned. "Imagine having someone like that teaching you at uni? A real-life spy who spent the last thirty years living in exile? Very cool."

"That would be cool," Leo agreed. "I'd have definitely paid more attention."

"How did you figure all that out?" Allissa asked, glancing at Leo. They stopped at a traffic light in a flurry of screeching brakes. Leo looked at Allissa.

"I don't really know, it just sort of... occurred to me. She was saying all this stuff, using all these words that didn't make sense. Plus, it felt like we'd been set up since the moment we arrived. Do you know what I mean?"

Allissa nodded. "It's impressive. I've obviously taught you —"

"No you haven't," Leo interrupted, smiling at Allissa.

The light turned green, and the traffic started to move. Looking at Allissa, Leo didn't notice. The car behind them honked. Leo tried to pull away. The Panda stuttered and stalled. The car behind them beeped again.

Allissa turned and held up her middle finger to the irate driver behind them. Leo restarted the engine. A cloud of thick black smoke belched from the back. The driver pulled into the other lane and sped past them in a stream of dust.

"Arsehole," Allissa muttered. She turned and glanced at the collection of parking tickets on the backseat. "How many parking tickets did you get while we were away?"

"Well, that's the thing —"

"How many?"

"You see, I thought they would only give me one. I was working on the theory that once you had one, the wardens would just leave the car alone —"

Allissa laughed out loud. "How many did you get?"

"Seven."

"Seven parking tickets! That's got to be almost more than this rust bucket is worth."

"Yeah, I worked it out. One more ticket and it would have been cheaper to let them tow the thing away."

Allissa's phone beeped. She dug it from her pocket and swiped it open.

"Message from Emilija. She says to put the radio on. Does the radio work?"

"Of course." Leo thumbed the button, and Allissa selected the station. A news channel was reporting on Mikhail's trial. Several members of the Latvian government had already been implicated, and many others had voluntarily stepped down in fear of what might go public.

Leo and Allissa listened in silence. They passed the Brighton Pavilion on one side and then the Palace Pier on the other. The seafront stretched out before them now, running into a hazy nothingness beyond the spire of the i360.

The news report came to an end as they turned from the seafront.

"You never know," Allissa said, clicking the radio off. "Maybe Emilija will end up running the country."

"I wouldn't rule anything out," Leo said, pulling into their street and slowing to a crawl. "Yes, get in! Look at that!" Leo shouted, index finger pointing through the windscreen.

Allissa squinted up the street and saw the cause of Leo's excitement. There was a vacant parking space right outside their flat.

Leo thumped the accelerator, and the car leapt forwards. He swung the wheel and slid straight into the vacant space.

"I told you it wasn't that bad having a car in the city. We've got a space right outside."

"Seven parking tickets," Allissa retorted, clambering out of the car.

"Yep, we're still in profit." Leo pulled up the windows, locked the doors and followed Allissa towards the building.

"That's not really the way it works," Allissa said, unlocking the communal door and leading them inside.

The air in the flat was thick and heavy. Allissa hoisted the sash windows upwards, disturbing several seagulls, and wedged various books beneath the decrepit windows to prevent them from slamming shut again.

Leo followed Allissa into the front room and dropped his bag on his desk.

"How impressed were you with my mental prowess?" he asked as Allissa turned.

"I've already told you it was impressive."

"Well, yeah, but you could tell me again. I'm not used to you saying nice things." Leo crossed the room and put his arms around Allissa. He pulled her in close. His heart beat heavily in his chest. He looked out at the street through the window. He took a deep breath and focused on the words he wanted to say.

"There's something I've been wanting to tell you," Leo said, pulling back and looking at Allissa. "I... I... I love —"

Leo's words caught in his throat as he noticed something through the window. A traffic warden crossed the road, pealed a parking ticket from his hand-held machine and slapped it to the windscreen of Leo's golden Fiat Panda.

"Oh, you've got to be... I just don't... you —" Leo shouted through the open window.

"I love you too," Allissa said, stepping in and silencing Leo's futile protests with a kiss. "But please get rid of that awful car."

READ ISTANBUL NOW

GOVERNMENTS IN CHAOS. **Violence in the streets. A new world order is coming.**

When Brent Fasslane, an exiled American conspiracy theorist, disappears in Istanbul, no one's surprised. Afterall, if you're a thorn in the side of the establishment, it's a matter of when, not if.

But, when the attention of the world's media sends Fasslane's new book up the charts, the powerful start to worry. A damning account of corruption within the world's governments, the book fuels a demand for change, with fear, violence, and bloodshed not far behind.

Leo and Allissa head to Istanbul in an attempt to prevent all out anarchy. But, when sinister forces intervene, it's clear the ancient city won't make it easy for them. Afterall, this wouldn't be the first-time civilisations have fallen in the labyrinthine streets of old Byzantium.

Can Leo and Allissa find the world's most famous missing person, before order crumbles for good?

**'Istanbul' is the most explosive of Luke Richardson's international thrillers to date. Pre-order your copy to find out why...**

READ ISTANBUL NOW

# WHAT HAPPENED IN KOH TAO?

READ THE SERIES PREQUEL NOVELLA FOR FREE NOW

★★★★★

"Intense, thrilling, mysterious and captivating."

★★★★★

"The story grabs you, you're on the boat with your stomach pitching. As the story gathers pace the tension is palpable.

It's a page turner which keeps you hooked until the final word."

★★★★★ "

The evocative writing takes you to a place of white sand, the turquoise sea and tranquilly. But on an island of injustice and exploitation, tranquillity is the last thing Leo finds."

★★★★★

"Love and adventure collide in Thailand, love it!"

**KOH TAO**

Leo's looking for the perfect place to propose to the love of his life. When they arrive in the Thai tropical paradise of Koh Tao, he thinks he's found it.

But before he gets an answer, she's nowhere to be seen.

On searching the resort, his tranquillity turns to turmoil. Is it a practical joke? Has she run away? Or is it something much more sinister?

Set two years before Luke Richardson's international thriller series, this compulsive novella turns back the clock on an anxiety ridden man battling powerful forces in a foreign land.

KOH TAO is the prequel novella to Luke Richardson's international thriller series. Grab your copy for free and find out where it all began!

READ THE SERIES PREQUEL NOVELLA FOR FREE NOW

*Books are difficult to write. Anyone who tells you differently is lying.*

*Not a month goes by where I don't think it's "too hard," or "not worth it." Every time this happens — as though by magic — I get an email from a reader like you.*

*Some are simple messages of encouragement, others are heartfelt, each one shows me that I'm not doing this alone.*

*If you've ever reached out to me, this book is dedicated to you. I appreciate the messages more than you'll ever know. They've kept me going when all seemed lost, and given me purpose when I didn't see it myself.*

*hello@lukerichardsonauthor.com*

# JOIN MY MAILING LIST

During the years it took me to write plan my first book, I always looked to its publication as being the end of the process. The book would be out, and the story would be finished.

Since releasing Kathmandu in May 2019, and then all my subsequent books, I realised that putting the story into the world was actually just the start. Now I go on the adventure with every conversation I have about it.

Most of these conversations happen with people on my mailing list, and I'd love you to join too.

I send an email a couple of times a month in which I talk about my new releases, my inspirations and my travels.

**Sign up now:**

www.lukerichardsonauthor.com/mailinglist

# THANK YOU

Thank you for reading *Riga*. Sharing my writing with you has been a dream of many years. Thank you for making it a reality.

As may come across in my writing, travelling, exploring and seeing the world is so important to me, as is coming home to my family and friends.

Although the words here are my own, the characters, experiences and some of the events described are wholly inspired by the people I've travelled beside. If we shared noodles from a street-food vendor, visited a temple together, played cards on a creaking overnight train, or chatted over beer in a back-street restaurant, you are forever in this book.

It is the intention of my writing to show that although the world is big and the unknown can be unsettling, there is so much good in it. Although some of the people in my stories are bad and evil — the story wouldn't be very interesting if they weren't — they're vastly outnumbered by the honesty, purity and kindness of the other characters. You don't have to look far to see this in the real world. I know that whenever I travel, it's the kindness of the people that I remember almost more than the place itself. Whether you're an experienced traveller, or you prefer your home turf, it's my hope that this story has taken you somewhere new and exciting.

Again, thank you for coming on the adventure with me. I hope to see you again soon.

Luke

PS. A little warning, next time someone talks to you in the airport, be careful what you say, as you may end up in their book.

# BOOK REVIEWS

If you've enjoyed this book I would appreciate a review.

Reviews are essential for three reasons. Firstly, they encourage people to take a chance on an author they've never heard of. Secondly, bookselling websites use them to decide which books to recommend through their search engine. And third, I love to hear what you think!

Having good reviews really can make a massive difference to new authors like me.

It'll take you no longer than two minutes, and will mean the world to me.

www.lukerichardsonauthor.com/reviews

Thank you.